D1564015

WHERE WOLVES DON'T DIE

WHERE WOLVES DON'T DIE

ANTON TREUER

LQ

LEVINE QUERIDO

MONTCLAIR · AMSTERDAM · HOBOKEN

This is an Arthur A. Levine book

Published by Levine Querido

LQ

LEVINE QUERIDO

www.levinequerido.com • info@levinequerido.com

Levine Querido is distributed by Chronicle Books, LLC

Library of Congress Control Number: 2023940111

ISBN 978-1-64614-381-8

Printed and bound in China

MIX
Paper | Supporting
responsible forestry
FSC
www.fsc.org
FSC® C144853

Published in June 2024

First Printing

For my son Caleb—the courageous.
Growth is not a springtime flood,
but a dance for all your seasons.
Play the music loud.

Northeast

Chapter 1

I HATED THE SNOW in Northeast Minneapolis. It looked pretty when it was falling from the sky, sometimes in large gentle flakes that made you want to stick out your tongue to catch them and sometimes whipping in harsh winds across the Plains and into the city, where the houses and stores and police station couldn't shield you. But the problem with the snow in Northeast Minneapolis wasn't the snow—it was Northeast Minneapolis. When the snow was falling from the sky, humans hadn't been able to taint it yet. But once it hit the ground, it started to melt and turn to slush and refreeze and change to ice. It made you slip and slide and forced you to walk differently, more carefully than you should have to. People spilled coffee in the snow. The dogs pooped and peed. Exhaust from the cars turned it gray. It never stayed pretty for long in Northeast.

There was only one thing that I really liked about where we lived—sitting in my ninth-grade biology class with Mr. Lukas next to Nora George. Nora was like the snow still falling from the sky. Sometimes she glided gently into the room and settled in her chair, with the grace of a Canadian lynx prowling for snowshoe hares. And sometimes she blew in fast and unpredictable, bumping into my desk or dropping her notebook. She had dark brown skin and long, shiny black hair that fell all the way to her waist. She might have seemed shy to others, but I had seen her at powwows with a tight red jingle dress and her eagle fan, beaming smiles as she bounced to the beat of the drum, raising her fan high in her long, slender fingers for the honor beats. She could light up any room in a heartbeat.

Nora's dark brown eyes held mine as she sat down. We had been friends since we were babies, but lately I felt like a deer in car headlights when she glanced my way.

I pointed at the textbook and spoke a little too fast, raising my eyebrows too: "We're going to start any second." I hoped it seemed like I was nervous about class.

Nora smiled and slowly started to pull books out of her backpack. I turned back to my book, relieved. She wasn't shy in the insecure way, and didn't cover it with too much makeup or perfume. She had a quiet confidence, like she knew things she would only share with a special few. For whatever reason, she liked to talk to me.

"Ezra. What section are we on?" Nora and I were both good students, but she was better at math. I liked to read. Today she was wearing tight blue jeans and white high-top basketball shoes. Her hair was loose, cascading over her neck and down a brand-new blue Toronto Maple Leafs hoodie.

My own shoes were scuffed from numerous skateboarding fails. I had a vintage Royce Gracie Ultimate Fighting Championship tee shirt on and baggy jeans. My head had jumped up a bit from the book at her question. I brushed my bangs from my eyes. I was still getting used to dealing with them: I had cut my long hair a year ago and had kept it short ever since.

"Chapter 2, section 8—trophic levels and keystone species," I replied.

"Keystone species? Oh yeah, the wolf section. But what would you know about that, Ezra?"

I was back to feeling like a deer in the headlights. Nora was messing with me. She knew I was wolf clan like my dad, and his dad, and all our Cloud family ancestors before that. We were one of the smallest families from Nigigoonsiminikaaning First Nation in Canada, but we knew who we were. In English, everyone called our rez "Red Gut," after the bay on Rainy Lake on the Ontario side of the Ontario-Minnesota border, where the village was. But the Ojibwe name literally meant "the place where there are a lot of little otter berries." It was a six-hour drive from Northeast Minneapolis to Red Gut. My body may have been stuck in Northeast, but my heart was always on the rez, fishing for walleyes, crappies, and smallmouth bass with my Grandpa Liam.

"Aren't you eagle clan, Nora?"

"Who wants to know? Your Grandpa Liam?" She smiled and opened her book.

I blushed. Dating someone of the same clan would be like dating a brother or sister. My grandpa liked to say that if someone wanted to go out with someone, skip digging for someone's horoscope sign, and instead ask, "Hey, baby, what's your clan?" He teased even harder than Nora. *I walked right into that one*, I thought.

"Ezra Cloud!"

I hadn't even noticed Mr. Lukas staring at me straight down the aisle. He wore a brown blazer, white collared shirt, blue jeans, and dress shoes. He didn't wear a watch or ring, but his short fingers were meticulously manicured. He had dark-rimmed glasses and a mop of brown hair, with a few streaks of gray, that made him look bookish and nerdy. I liked nerds. The entire class shifted to look at me.

"Ezra Cloud. What are keystone species?"

Mr. Lukas had caught me flat-footed, so I shuffled my feet and hesitated. But I knew the answer.

"A keystone species is a species that all the other animals in an ecosystem depend on. The entire ecosystem would change without it."

"That's right. Can you give us an example?"

I had done my homework. "The jaguar and the timber wolf are both keystone species and apex predators. They order their entire ecosystems because their hunting and movement patterns change the behavior of all other animals in their systems. The beaver is a keystone, but not an apex predator, because it's an ecosystem engineer."

Mr. Lukas nodded and turned to the white board. It wasn't until then that the sneering voice finally sounded one desk behind me, as predictable as the city traffic, sirens, and smog.

"I bet you think you're smarter than everyone else, don't you, Ezra?" the voice hissed. "You might fool Mr. Lukas once in a while, but you can't fool the rest of us. You're just another dumb Indian, Ezra."

I turned around to look at Matt Schroeder. I hated him even more than all the dirty snow in Northeast

Minneapolis. He was wearing his usual—weathered Timberland boots, loose blue jeans, and a flannel shirt. He kept his hair in a greasy blond mullet. Mr. Lukas made him keep his baseball hat off in class, but it was a regular fixture the rest of the time. I bet he slept with it on.

Goose bumps rippled up my neck. "Shut up, Matt!" I snapped.

Matt smelled like a mechanic at the end of a long day in the shop: body odor mixed with engine oil. But everyone in Northeast knew they weren't fixing cars at the Schroeder house. They were fixing up something else.

"Shut up, or what?" Matt was smiling now. He was fifteen years old—the same as me—but his teeth were gross. I should have felt sorry for him, I suppose. He was a victim of his environment. But, at fifteen years of age, I couldn't escape the way he treated me.

I kept staring him down. There was a line of thin blond stubble around his upper lip, pulled back into sneer. It must have given him some sick pleasure to know that he could still get under my skin. Whenever I looked at Matt, I imagined him a couple years older, with a regular mustache and blue military uniform. He was just the kind of colonizer who would've been a perfect fit in the US 7th Cavalry in 1890, trying to kill innocent Lakota children with a Hotchkiss gun. And my imagination wasn't even that far from the truth.

Instead of bullets, Matt and his family were cooking up meth in their basement. They were taking lives all the same.

I knew that someday he would mess up. I should have been satisfied with the knowledge that Matt would likely be dead from a drug overdose eventually, or the explosion of a meth lab, or locked in prison until he was too old to have babies. But I couldn't avoid fantasizing about what a pleasure it would be to kill him myself— like the Lakota did to Custer back in 1876.

I turned back around and did my best to ignore him. Nora gave me a cautionary glance too, so I opened my textbook to follow Mr. Lukas. But I wasn't smiling.

Nora knew me well, but she didn't know everything. I was six feet tall now and weighed one hundred and eighty-five pounds, which made me one of the biggest kids in the ninth grade—probably thirty pounds heavier than Matt. But I had done a lot of my growing recently. Two years before, Matt was a little bigger than me. We'd ended up on a canoe trip together with a summer camp for boys in northern Minnesota. Since I was an only child, my dad thought it would be good for me to have a social experience with kids my own age, in the great outdoors. But I was the only Native kid on that trip. And that wasn't cool there.

Matt wasn't the only one who had a lot to learn about us. We paddled out into the middle of nowhere where the boreal forest of black spruce, jack pine, and birch lined pristine waterways, where you could still drink the water right out of the lakes and set up camp. Everyone sat around the fire, getting ready to eat some mac and cheese. That's when Matt walked up to me and slapped me across the face as hard as he could, swearing at me and calling me names. He started with "damn Indian," and it only got worse from there. The camp counselors were right there and they didn't even try to stop him. The other kids started to laugh. I walked away until there was nobody in sight and started to cry. It took me a while to regain my composure.

The counselors said that Matt and I would have to sleep in the same tent and figure out how to get along. Get along? I was assaulted and they hadn't even said it was wrong, much less punished him. So, our first night in that tent, I waited until Matt was sleeping, then I unzipped the tent door and found a hefty, five-pound rock. I grabbed it in both hands and held it a couple feet above his upturned, sleeping face. I was so close to smashing that rock into his nose. I'm embarrassed to admit it now, but what stopped me was not a sense that it would be immoral. I was simply afraid that if I didn't succeed in killing him, he would kill me instead. My parents wouldn't even have been likely to get my body back. So I put the rock outside. And I suffered his company the rest of the trip. I never told my parents. I never told Nora, or anybody else. I'd take that secret with me to the grave. But I never forgot.

Nora's voice pulled me back out of my head. "Overharvesting of keystone species, climate change, or disease could cause trophic cascade and change the entire ecosystem."

"That's right." Mr. Lukas seemed pleased. "Disease patterns are getting a lot of attention now. For tomorrow, I want all of you to watch one of the news reports about new virus patterns and be prepared to discuss the role of humans in accelerating or slowing down ecosystem collapse."

The bell sounded so we started to shuffle out of the classroom. I was glad to be moving around. Sitting at a desk was not my love language.

"Ezra, are you okay?" Nora muttered over the roar of voices. "You seemed lost in a daydream for half the class." She looked curious, maybe even concerned.

"Oh. Sorry about that. I guess I was."

Matt strode past us without a word, for once, and got lost in the crowd spilling into the hallway. I waited for Nora to methodically repack her backpack. Her long hair kept rolling from her shoulders to her books. She stood and slung her backpack across her left shoulder, finally letting it flow over and around it.

"Don't worry about Matt. He's a punk and everyone who's anyone knows."

I smiled. She always knew what to say.

Chapter 2

I HAD TO GET to algebra next. Mrs. Byrne wore comfortable black dress shoes and a pink business suit that clashed with her bright red hair. It must have naturally been pretty flat and straight, but the world would never know for sure because she'd kept it in a tightly curled perm as long as anyone could remember. She usually had us tackle worksheets and calculate equations from the text.

Thankfully, Matt was too dumb for algebra, so I didn't have to deal with him for another hour. But Nora had World History at the same time, and I wouldn't see her until the end of the school day. It was a little lonely without her sitting in the desk next to me. So I did what

I usually did when I was left to myself, and started thinking about my other secrets.

Everyone knew that my mom, Isabelle, died a year ago. She used to work at Erickson Lumber Company, one of the last wood treatment plants in the Twin Cities. She often had to handle the chemicals for the wood treatment in the pulp plant. She ended up getting acute lymphoblastic leukemia and died within months of her diagnosis. ELC never took responsibility for how their chemicals might have caused my mom's cancer, but it was hard to imagine it being anything else.

What everyone didn't know was that every time I thought about my mom, my mind went blank. I couldn't follow a conversation, read a book, or even talk about it. I could hardly remember her funeral. I tried to look at old family photos and could sometimes remember her teaching me to ride a bike or getting me to line up for grand entry at the summer powwows, but the memories seemed so faint and long ago. I preferred not to think about her because that made it easier for me to function, but it still felt like there was a black hole where she had been, and it was closing in on me.

Usually, Nora and I chatted about movies and television shows, her powwow regalia (she was an expert beader), Minecraft, stuff like that. Her dad died when she was just three years old, so she told me she understood what I was going through, and that she was there if I ever wanted to talk about it. But she couldn't really understand. She hardly knew her dad. My mom had been everything to me.

After we learned that my mom had leukemia, I got a big electric fan from the basement and turned it on full blast in my room to make white noise, so I didn't have to hear my parents talking about chemotherapy or hear them crying at night. But I couldn't drown out the fact that I was scared.

My dad kept a pouch of tobacco on the kitchen counter. We used tobacco not to chew or smoke, but as an offering when we prayed. We put some tobacco on the ground when we harvested blueberries on the rez back at Red Gut. We put some in the water when we harvested fish. Offering tobacco was like saying, "We aren't just taking things, we are exchanging an offering for food." And we used it when we prayed, putting tobacco by a tree or a rock, like saying, "In exchange for hearing this prayer, we offer this tobacco." At some ceremonies they did smoke it in a pipe, but my dad said I couldn't do that until after I went fasting.

So one night I cranked up the fan in my room, took a pinch of the tobacco in my hand, put the pouch on my nightstand, and I prayed. I prayed that my mom wouldn't suffer and that she would stop crying. I put the tobacco from my hand on the windowsill and drifted off to sleep.

I made that tobacco offering in November. By the following November, I never heard my parents crying any more, but it wasn't because everything got better. My mom was gone. She would never show up for school things for me again. There were no more chore lists on the fridge every Sunday.

My memories of her sickness and funeral were more like pictures than full memories. I could remember her coughing blood into Kleenex in the bathroom one time, but she rushed to shut the door. I could remember standing by her hospital bed while she slept late at night, looking gray and skinny and bald from her chemotherapy, until my dad told me to take a nap in the waiting room.

I remembered the place we buried her at the mouth of the Ottertail River at Red Gut. She was enrolled at the White Earth Reservation in Minnesota, but she had been raised in foster homes. She'd wanted to be buried where my dad's family was. I didn't say anything after we got home from the funeral. I just went upstairs, down the hallway and into my room.

I turned on the fan like I usually did and started to wonder. Why had I prayed that my mom would stop crying? Prayer answered. But it just made everything worse. Why did my dad have to be a professor? Why did we have to live in Northeast Minneapolis with all of its dirty snow? Why couldn't we just move back to Red Gut, so I could hunt and trap do the things our family had always done? I was from a long line of trappers and hunters, but I never even had a chance to trap or hunt for deer or moose because the hunting season was in the fall, and trapping was in the winter, and I was always in Northeast going to school. Why couldn't my dad use his big, brown warrior hands to be a warrior? Warriors protect. It was his job to protect our family—to protect my mom, even from cancer. To protect me. But he failed. They all failed.

I was mad now. Mad at my mom for dying. Mad at my dad for not saving her. Mad at our neighborhood. I still had the pouch of tobacco from the kitchen on my nightstand and took another pinch. I prayed again. I prayed that we wouldn't have to live here anymore. I prayed that my dad would be a strong protector like he was supposed to be. I prayed that I'd see my mom again. I prayed that everything would be okay. And I prayed that I wouldn't have to feel ashamed of my family and all our problems. I prayed myself to sleep, the tobacco slipping from hand to the bedsheets and the floor.

"Ezra Cloud, can I see your worksheet, please?" Mrs. Byrne was standing at my desk. I had no idea how long I had been wrapped up in my thoughts, but she seemed disappointed to find an empty worksheet on top of my notebook.

"I'm sorry, Mrs. Byrne. I'm not feeling that great."

"You'll be feeling a whole lot less great if you don't make some progress on that worksheet, Ezra. Get your head in the classroom and on those problem sets." I scribbled frenetically at the paper for the rest of class. It wasn't my best performance, but better than nothing.

I shuffled into the hallway afterwards, my jaw clenched now and my hands in fists. I was normally pretty easygoing, but at this point I was feeling like I just wanted to punch something, or someone.

I turned the hallway corner by my locker bay just in time to see Matt Schroeder smack the stack of books out of Nora's hand. The books scattered and fell to the floor; she quickly bent down to pick them up. Matt hovered over her with a sneer across his face, his baseball hat hiding his eyes. His engine oil and body odor stench clung to him all the way from here, like the perfume of old white women walking in the Mall of America—inescapable and obtrusive.

"You look kind of pretty down there on the floor, Nora," Matt spat. "That must be right where you belong."

"You're a pig, Matt. Leave me alone." Her voice shook with emotion.

Nora left the books on the floor and rose to her feet. She was a lot smaller than Matt, but seemed utterly fearless as she faced him. He grabbed her, his long, pale fingers encircling her entire wrist, pulling her close.

"You should come to my place after school so we can finish this conversation." He was actually enjoying this. The frozen shock that'd gripped me at first melted to the floor.

I was bounding down the hallway towards Matt and Nora faster than a wolf on a whitetail deer. Matt wheeled to face me, a big, yellow smile across his face. I wasn't even thinking now. I just saw red. I must have looked as angry as I felt because a crowd of teenagers, eager to witness some drama, closed quickly around us.

"I dare you to hit me, you stupid Indian." Matt smirked from under his baseball cap and pointed at the rows of onlooking students. "We have a hallway full of witnesses, and they'll *all* dime you out. You can spend the rest of high school in a juvenile detention center. Or better yet, they'll try you as an adult! Then you can go to prison with one of your deadbeat cousins."

Nora twisted her wrist and popped it out of his hand. She circled beside me and I moved a foot in front of her.

"Ezra. Don't hit him. It isn't worth it." Her voice was tense and strained.

Matt laughed.

The throng of kids surrounding us grew, and out of the corner of my eye, I saw Mr. Lukas striding quickly down the hallway toward the pack of kids. Matt just folded his arms across his chest and stuck out his stubbled chin. My blood boiled.

I knew that my clenched fist could knock Matt straight to the ground. I sucked in all my breath in an effort at self-control, Nora's words echoing in my ear. Then I let out an enraged growl and smashed a punch into the locker next to his pasty face. Matt jumped to the side, and I stepped back. I'd hit the locker with such force that it caved in the locker door, rupturing the hinge on one side and popping the paint off the center of the door.

Mr. Lukas hollered from down the hall and kids started to scatter in all directions. Matt laughed at me, unperturbed, his voice full of gravel and ice. He turned his head and winked at Nora one last time, then slowly strutted down the hallway.

"Your hand . . ." Nora's voice was soft but penetrating. She touched my arm and I looked at it, a big gash running from the knuckle on my index finger down to the wrist. It was swelling quickly and blood was pouring onto the floor.

Chapter 3

MY DAD WAS A big man—six feet three inches tall and probably weighing two hundred and fifty pounds. He was more muscle than fat and looked impressive, even imposing, as he stood in the doorway of the school nurse's office.

"Are you Byron Cloud?" Kayla Anderson, the school nurse, was a tall woman with dishwater-blond hair and a serious face. She wore new tennis shoes, blue stretch slacks, a tee shirt, and a white lab coat.

"I'm Byron Cloud." My dad stood unflinching just inside the doorway, but his eyes shifted from Mrs. Anderson to Nora and me. Nora and I had been waiting in the nurse's office for half hour while Mr. Lukas called my dad from the main office.

Mrs. Anderson shook her head as she finished wrapping up my wrist and hand. "Thanks for coming to the school so quickly, Mr. Cloud. This could be a serious break. I think you should get Ezra to the emergency room," she said.

The adrenaline was finally starting to abate and I could feel the pain pulsing and swelling in my hand and wrist. I was sweating and my lips trembled. I looked at my feet.

Mr. Lukas stuck his head in Mrs. Anderson's office. He might have been relieved he didn't have to try to separate a brawl between me and Matt, but he seemed nervous around my dad. He glanced over the top of his glasses and said with a weighty sigh, "I'll have to report the damage to the locker. This isn't over yet, I'm afraid." He wasn't unkind about it, and surely had no choice in the matter, but I decided then that I hated him. Even Nora's supportive presence couldn't shake me out of my murky mood.

For a second my mind flashed back to August, when I was pulling fish nets with my Grandpa Liam at the mouth of the Ottertail River and a large muskie got mixed in with the walleyes. The fish was so huge that it knocked me to the bottom of the canoe when I pulled it from the net and it started flopping. Grandpa Liam offered no help. He just sat right down in canoe, laughing at me.

My dad's voice pulled me back. "I'll get him to the emergency room for an X-ray. Let me know what kind of follow-up you need about the locker." He nodded at Mrs. Anderson and gestured to Mr. Lukas. His hands were huge—long, but thick and muscular too. They were perfectly suited for any of our ancestral duties—pulling fish nets, skinning moose, bending tamarack poles for wigwams. He came from generations of accomplished Native trappers, hunters, and warriors too.

I used to be amused that my dad chose for his profession the most indoor job imaginable. He was a professor and taught our tribal language, Ojibwe, at Minneapolis Community & Technical College. There were a lot of Ojibwe people in Minneapolis ever since the relocation program in the 1950s. A lot of them wanted to learn their language now.

But whenever my dad tried to type on the computer he got from the college, his big fingers would hit two keys with every keystroke. He actually had to order a special keyboard so he could function. He was big and formidable and brown. To me, he looked like a duck on dry land in the city—out of his element. But he loved our language, and he loved teaching, and his job paid the bills.

"Ezra and Nora, let's go," my dad said.

We followed him into the hallway out the door to the parking lot. My dad drove a Subaru Forester. He was an idealist when it came to love and the Ojibwe language, but practical about everything else. The Subaru had all-wheel drive and could handle the snow and the rougher terrain back on the rez, where we spent our summer months, and it was good on gas for city life the rest of the time. It was a few years old, but it didn't smell as bad as the rest of this city. I sat in the front. Nora hopped in the back.

My dad wore an insulated blue zip-up coat, his dress shirt visible at the collar. He gave me a concerned look but didn't say anything. Between my mood and the pain from my injury, I wouldn't have been much of a conversationalist anyways. He looked in the rearview mirror and spoke over the thrum of traffic: "Nora, I won't even bother asking him what happened. Can you fill me in?"

She gave him the whole story on our way to the Hennepin County Medical Center. HCMC is a huge medical complex with big parking ramps and a skyway connecting it to hotels and the labyrinth of shops and businesses in downtown Minneapolis. The whole place was surrounded by dirty snow. And full of stressed-out families, with every kind of drama and trauma.

It took them forever to sort me out. My dad might have been concerned about my hand, but as we sat in the waiting room, he seemed a lot more worried about my lack of self-control.

"Ezra, you have to be careful. Remember what happened to Michael and Jonah?"

"I remember."

My cousin Michael was shot by the police when he got pulled over on a routine traffic stop, visiting us in Northeast. He made it back to the rez in a coffin. My cousin Jonah had moved to Minneapolis for a few months. He got convicted of manslaughter with circumstantial evidence. He hadn't hurt anyone. But he was locked up, and would be for years to come.

"I need to know that you're going to be wise enough not to give the cops a reason to pull a gun out around you."

"They don't need a reason, Dad."

"That might be true. But when they have one, it's always worse."

My hand and wrist were throbbing now.

"You know it's not just the police," he said. "Remember what happened to Stanley?"

My cousin Stanley got beat up just going for a walk. He had only been in Northeast for two weeks. He was my Grandma Emma's sister's son. He actually made it back to the rez and was wise enough to stay. He was probably in his fifties now—too old for street fights, and never looking for trouble.

"I remember."

"I promised your mom that I'd keep you safe, Ezra."

I looked at the floor and mumbled, "I know."

"That Matt Schroeder lives only six blocks from us. I know his dad, Mark, and his Uncle Luke. Stay away from those people."

We could agree on that much at least.

Nora kept her head down while we talked, focused on her phone. The tension between me and my dad probably made her nervous. But our families knew each other well.

It wasn't purely coincidence that Nora and her mom, Ruth, had moved to the same neighborhood as my parents in Northeast. My dad helped Nora's mom find a job and a house in the city as a favor to his mom. Grandma Emma and Nora's Grandma Rita had been friends and neighbors for decades. I guess he showed them what he knew in the city. We'd all been there ever since.

After a couple of hours, I received eleven stitches and a removable cast because my fracture ran along one of the bones in my hand, rather than straight across, and it was non-displaced, meaning that they didn't have to reset any bones. It was supposed to be good news, but it didn't feel very good to me.

We dropped Nora off on our way home. She lived in a small ranch-style house several blocks from ours. Ruth was on the front steps with a long gray woolen coat on, waiting. Her white nurse shoes shifted nervously as we approached. She waved and it was uncanny how much she resembled her daughter, from her lithe figure to her long, slender fingers. Ruth looked stressed. I hadn't thought about how what had happened might have affected her.

Ruth's husband had fallen through the ice and died of hypothermia when Nora was just three years old. Ruth moved to the city for work, but they still went back to the rez often in the summer months to stay with her mother. It meant that I got to see even more of Nora, which was all I could hope for. But Nora was everything to Ruth and Rita, and it probably made them worry even more than most people did about their kids and grandkids. Nora gave me a wave as she slid out of the Subaru and glided up to her mom. My dad pulled away.

I was barely able to keep my anger under control by the time we pulled into our driveway. I used my right hand to unbuckle. I gingerly pulled my cast into a cradle to avoid bumping it as I got out of the car. I was mumbling under my breath, "I should teach him a proper lesson. I should kill him myself and do the world a favor."

My dad was right behind me and put his hand on my shoulder so I couldn't move forward. "Gwis. It's okay to be angry. And it's okay to say how angry you are. But making threats or acting on your anger can really make a mess out of your life."

"Maybe I'll just kill myself then," I blurted. I didn't really mean it, and I regretted it the second I said it. Maybe I just wanted my dad to do something about my whole life and everything that had gotten so messed up about it.

I could feel my dad's enormous body tensing behind me. He pulled me with enough force to spin me around to face him. "Gwis, I don't ever want to hear you say that again." Now there was a deeply pained look on his face.

He stared at me intently, but I just looked down at my cast and turned back to go inside. I stomped up the stairs to our house, kicked off my shoes, and went straight to my room.

My dad left me alone for a while. Once I calmed down, I felt bad for scaring him with my suicide comments. But I did wonder what it would be like to die. Would there be a tunnel? Would there be light or darkness? Would it hurt more or less than being alive?

I heard a knock at the door an hour or two later and then my dad appeared with a tray of food—venison stew, buttered bread—all easy enough to eat with one hand.

"How's the pain, gwis?"

"The pain is still painful."

"Here. You can take one of these when you're ready to go to sleep." He plucked out a Percocet and put it with a glass of water on the nightstand by my bed, but he took the rest of the bottle with him when he left the room. The doctor had prescribed the drug for the pain relief, but I knew it was so powerful that an overdose could kill you.

I went to the bathroom and brushed my teeth without toothpaste. I didn't want to try wrangling the top off with one hand, and it was too painful to manage with two. Back in my room, I shut the door with a sigh and fumbled into pajama bottoms and a fresh tee shirt. I popped the pill and drank the water, turned on the fan, and crawled under the covers. It felt like I left my body for a minute . . . falling through the floor, the kitchen below, the basement, and down, down, down.

Chapter 4

I WOKE SEVERAL HOURS LATER to the sound of footsteps outside my door. It seemed strange. My dad was a big man and his weight gave a distinctive creak to the floorboards. This sounded like someone else. Someone lighter? My room had carpet and I noiselessly slipped out of bed and to the door. Whoever it was, was still there. I slowly turned the handle of the doorknob and prepared to pop the door open quickly. But then I heard the footsteps darting away. Maybe they saw the door knob moving?

I flung the door open. It banged against the wall of my room and I whipped my head into the hallway. The corridor was dark, but was that a flash of movement? It was so fast. All I could be sure of were the colors—brown and gray. I'd been sure that I would be standing face-to-face with my dad, or someone I knew. But the hall was empty.

I was spooked. I wasn't sure why I spoke in a whisper, but I said, "Who's there?"

No response.

I wanted to go to my dad's room and ask him. I wanted to explore the house, maybe flick on all the lights and holler after the intruder. The hair on the back of my neck was standing on end. I was wearing my Naruto shirt and flannel pajama bottoms, suddenly aware of how vulnerable I would be if this was a home invasion—no protective clothes or weapons.

I just stood there for a few minutes in the silence, staring into the darkness of the hallway, then eventually figured it must be the Percocet messing with my head. I turned around and went back to bed.

But I lay under the covers for a while after, trying to process everything.

Finally, just as I was drifting back to sleep, I heard the faint sound of voices coming from the kitchen below. The fan was drowning out the details, so I crawled out of bed and shut it off.

There was definitely someone in the house. It couldn't be an intruder, because it sounded like they were talking to my dad. My dad's voice had a distinct baritone, and he was definitely in the conversation. But the other voice was a man with a higher-pitched voice. He sounded older. It reminded me of my grandfather. But it couldn't be Grandpa Liam. My grandparents *never* came down to the Twin Cities. I didn't even know if they knew how. They always stayed on the rez at Red Gut, or in the woods, unless they were shopping in Fort Frances nearby. I didn't even think they had passports, or smartphones. Maybe it was Daniel Drumbeater? Daniel was a friend of ours, and actually chief of Nigigoonsiminikaaning First Nation, the one who gave me my Native name as a kid. He named me Anangoowinini, meaning Star Man. Sometimes, when he had business in Minneapolis, he came to the house to visit with me. Namesakes are spiritual guides, role models, and protectors.

I moved to the door and carefully opened it again, but it creaked suddenly and I heard the conversation in the kitchen stop immediately. Now they were listening for me. If it was Daniel Drumbeater or Grandpa Liam, I would have been thrilled to see them. But . . . wouldn't they have come to see me instead of being secretive? And they wouldn't be stopping by in the middle of the night. *Maybe it's the police*, I thought. But could that be true? I stood there for a while, mulling things over once more, and I don't remember what happened next but I must have stepped back in the room and gone back to sleep. I do remember thinking: *I really must be imagining things.*

I had a powerful dream that night. In my dream I was running with a pack of wild timber wolves. I was howling like they were, and we were chasing something. I was in my own body, but had all the senses of a wolf. I could smell the damp sphagnum moss, the earthy spores of the mushrooms, the piney scent of the black spruce— and also the scent of the animals, white tail deer, the vapor trail from their tarsal glands penetrating my nasal cavity and filling me with energy and hunger. I felt so alive, so powerful.

And then the scene switched and we were hunting in the city. Now the smell of diluted urine in the streets, car exhaust, and dogs covered the ground, and the scent of human pheromones filled the air, acrid and intrusive. But instead of chasing the deer, now we were chasing Matt Schroeder through the alleys and streets, his skin pallid and greasy in the streetlight, with a look of fear so palpable we could smell it.

Our pack chased him into a dilapidated house in Northeast Minneapolis, then circled his refuge. My heart was racing, knowing he'd finally get his lesson. We covered all the doors and windows. I reached into my pocket for a lighter and lit a torch, tossing it in the front door and slamming it shut. I stood back and watched as the fire slowly spread and then muffled screams erupted inside. The blaze caught the drapes and licked along the ceiling. Dark smoke started to billow out from the edges of the doors and roof vents, but the screams eventually died and the inferno raged larger, until the heat burst the windows and engulfed the house in flames. I watched with the pack, in satisfied silence, until we heard the police and fire crews start to come down. Then we trotted away and suddenly were back in the forest, lying down among the trees.

I WOKE SLOWLY, NOT knowing where I was at first. *That was the best dream I ever had*, I thought to myself. It had felt so real, so much so that I could still smell the faint tingle of smoke in my nose. I smiled. I looked around, only realizing then that I wasn't in my bed. I was on the floor, clammy sweat across my skin. My heart was beating like a drum.

I felt a momentary pang of guilt about how good that dream felt. I sat up and pulled my knees to my chest. *It was just a dream*, I thought. *A good dream.*

I felt a little lighter as I grabbed a change of clothes with my good hand and glided down the hallway to the bathroom. The Percocet had worn off, and I noticed that my hand was throbbing, a little blood soaking through the bandage. I donned one of the plastic shower gloves they'd given me for my bandage, cranked the spigot, and pulled the stopper, bracing myself against the shower wall as I stepped in. I always noticed how the water in Minneapolis had a faint difference in taste from the shallow well at my grandparents' house in Red Gut—likely from the big city's water treatment plant. My mind was awash in conflicting thoughts about my exhilarating dream, anger toward Matt Schroeder, and unexpected melancholy about my mom that seemed to hit me every now and then for no reason. The water hit my face and ran down my body, as warm as tears. When I finished, I used my right hand to work the towel and slipped into my jeans and tee shirt. I descended the stairs then, ravenous.

My dad was cooking, his large frame testing the merits of his weekend clothes—jeans and a Redbone tee shirt—as he bent over the stove. He turned when I sat at the table and gave me a piercing stare. I thought maybe my somewhat lighter mood this morning might rub off on him, but he seemed pretty determined and serious still, even more than I expected, so I didn't say a word even though there was a lot on my mind. My old man was a decent cook, and I did some of my best work eating that breakfast, wolfing down three pancakes, four eggs, bacon, and a tall glass of orange juice. I could tell my gusto didn't go unnoticed.

Part of me wanted to tell him everything—about Matt and me at summer camp and the rock, how my mind went blank whenever I tried to think about Mom, that it felt like darkness was closing in on me sometimes.

I wanted to tell him about my strange dream too. He might be able to make sense of it. My dad and my Grandpa Liam were close. They both spoke Ojibwe, and I heard them talking about spiritual things many times—how they saw us not as humans having occasional spiritual experiences, but as spirits having temporary human experiences. We didn't have souls. We were souls who have bodies for a little while. Maybe he could decipher it. But I was still too mad. It was his job to take care of us, and from where I was sitting, he was doing a terrible job. He couldn't protect my mom from cancer. He could have convinced her to work somewhere else—anywhere but Erickson Lumber. He couldn't protect me from Matt.

He couldn't protect any of us from the cops, juvenile detention centers, and prisons. I was one wrong punch from a lifetime of that. White people didn't have to live with that kind of fear the way we did. *He* was the one who made us live in Northeast Minneapolis, and I hated this place. I hated my school. This house didn't feel like home. This city didn't feel like home. But he made us stay. For his job. We used to stay for mom's job too. Now it was just for the memory of her.

"I need to talk to you, Ezra."

Of course he did. The big breakfast wasn't just him being a nice dad. He wanted to open me up about why I was punching lockers at school.

"Son, are you aware of what happened last night?"

My mind started racing. Was it about the voices I heard last night, or the person I thought I heard outside of my room? Was there a home invasion and I was too out of it to notice? Had the cops come? Were they going to press charges against me for destruction of school property?

"Son, I love you, and I am on your side no matter what."

This conversation was heading in an ominous direction.

"I need to know if you stayed in your room all night last night."

Maybe the conversation I'd heard *wasn't* with him— maybe he'd heard the voices too, or saw someone sneaking around?

"Answer me."

"Yeah. I stayed in my room, Dad."

He seemed relieved, but his brow was still furrowed and his clumsy hands fidgeted with his coffee cup. He was uncharacteristically nervous.

"Gwis, the Schroeders died last night."

My heart started pounding in my chest so hard that I was sure he could hear it. Was my dream just a dream? Or some distorted version of the truth?

"How?"

As I asked the question, I thought I might already know the answer, or some version of it. He looked at me quizzically. His shoulders tensed and he gave the coffee cup a spin before he replied. "Matt's father, Mark, died. So did his Uncle Luke. Matt survived, but barely. I guess they had a meth lab going in their basement. It started a fire last night and the whole house went up in flames, with all three of them inside."

Chapter 5

TWENTY MINUTES LATER, my smartphone was buzzing like the subwoofers at the Toronto SkyDome Powwow. Messages were flooding in from Nora, Noah, Oliver, Amelia, and some other friends at school asking if I'd heard the news. The modern-day moccasin telegram was mainly full of curiosity seekers, but Nora was freaking out.

Did you hear about the Schroeders? About the fire? OMG, I'm FR freaking out, Ezra. Meet me behind the BK on Central. It was the last in over a dozen messages she'd sent.

OMW! I replied. The Burger King on Central reflected our neighborhood—too many people, not enough money. And Northeast wasn't the worst part of

Minneapolis. North Minneapolis was even more run-down than Northeast. We were in a tug-of-war between gentrifying hipsters on one side, and the steady swirl of the desperate and disenfranchised on the other.

Nora was standing at the edge of the parking lot when I got there. Her hair was pulled into a tight ponytail, and she wore a zip-up puffer jacket with a Maple Leafs beanie and matching mittens. She looked cute sporting some Canadian pride, but the stress lines on her face were real.

"Thanks for coming, Ezra. You're such a good friend." *Friend.* Despite everything I felt that moment, I still couldn't help wishing she could see me as more than that.

"Ezra, walk with me." Her eyes seemed to dart around and I could feel the tension in her voice. We started to walk down the sidewalk as she continued, "Do you think we are in trouble? After what happened at school, the cops might think we both had motive to burn Matt's house. When white people die, someone gets punished. Even if it's really sketchy white people like Mark and Luke Schroeder."

"Nora, we didn't kill anybody. It was an accident and neither of us were there." I wasn't one hundred percent sure of that, but I wasn't ready to talk about my dream and the people in our house and what was real and what wasn't.

We walked down Central for a couple of blocks more and turned. The streets in that part of Northeast were all named after American presidents—Harrison, Tyler. None of them would have set foot in our neighborhood if they could transport through time. When we were about a block and half from the Schroeder residence, and about to turn into the alley that led there, I pulled her aside.

"Nora, I don't think we should be here. If someone sees us, they might get the wrong idea."

"We won't get too close. Let's just see what's going on." She sounded anxious but determined.

I reluctantly followed her further down the alley. There was still a strong smell of smoke in the air. And as we neared the Schroeder place, we could see emergency vehicles everywhere. The firefighters were dousing the smoldering remains of the house. Police officers had the entire area blocked off with caution tape and there were a few of them with notepads talking to neighbors, collecting statements. The fire had left the snow melted away from the remains of the house and covered everywhere else around in dark gray soot.

"You're right, Nora. They're investigating. Do you think it was arson?"

"It doesn't matter what I think. It matters what *they* think." She pointed with her lips toward the burned-down house. Pointing with the lips was an Ojibwe custom and I couldn't help being charmed, in spite of the seriousness of what was happening.

"Well, it's almost Christmas break. We're going to Red Gut soon to be with my grandparents. You too?"

"Yeah, soon as school is out. I can't wait. They'll want to talk to us, Ezra. I hate talking to cops. I think they just look for excuses to get us in trouble."

"But if we didn't do anything wrong, we have nothing to hide." She didn't say anything in response, but we edged a little closer to get a better look at the house.

After a few minutes of watching, Nora turned me. Her eyes seemed to droop. "I feel sorry for Matt. He's still a kid: it was his dad and uncle that made him the way he is. He may be a first-class jerk, but he never had a chance to learn how to be decent, and now he probably never will. I bet they put him into foster care."

I wasn't feeling as gracious as Nora, but I kept my thoughts to myself. We watched the flurry of police activity for about fifteen minutes more before we decided to leave. But when we turned, a man was in the alley, blocking our path.

The guy wore a suit and dress coat and carried a clipboard and pen. He wasn't wearing a hat, which seemed a little unwise given the cold, but it didn't seem to bother him.

"Hello, my name is John Williams," he said, coming up to us. "I'm a detective investigating the fire." I felt unexpectedly dizzy. I wondered how long he'd been behind us, and what he might have heard. Part of me was a little relieved that Williams was Black. Maybe he'd be a little more sensitive to racial stereotyping, and Nora's concerns about unfair treatment would be unfounded.

"What are your names?"

"Ezra Cloud."

"I'm Nora George."

The detective started to jot down notes on his clipboard. "Did either of you know the people who lived at that house?" He glanced over our shoulders at the police and fire trucks behind us and the burned-down remains. Then a familiar voice shouted out to him. We turned to see my dad striding across the street from the other direction. His black winter puffer jacket swooshed as he closed in on Detective Williams, pulling a leather glove off his right hand and offering his bare hand to the detective.

"I'm Byron Cloud. Ezra is my son." He shook hands with Detective Williams.

"I was just asking the kids here a couple of questions. Is that okay with you, Mr. Cloud?"

My dad didn't even hesitate to respond: "No, it's not. These are minor children. We are happy to cooperate with the investigation, but I wish to be present when my son is questioned and I want our attorney, Paul Taylor, to be present as well. I am sure that Ruth George feels the same way about her daughter, Nora."

Detective Williams just raised an eyebrow and jotted a few more notes on his clipboard. "This fire is being investigated as an arson-homicide. We are interviewing all the Schroeder neighbors and associates. We will need statements from all three of you." He paused and stared at us, shifting his gaze from me to Nora to my dad. Williams handed a business card to my dad. "Call this number and make an appointment. Soon."

"We will."

Williams walked back across the street. My dad turned and started to walk down the alley. "Come on, kids. Let's get out of here."

Nora and I followed after my dad. I had a thousand questions running through my head. Arson? Homicide? How could they even know? The house was a pile of ash. Nora looked anxious too, but she didn't say anything.

Somewhere behind us a loud, gravelly voice penetrated my thoughts:

"Hey! Yeah, you!"

Nora and I turned around at the same time as my dad, who was still a few feet ahead of us. There was a figure standing in the alley with no coat on and bandages wrapped around his skull, arm, and chest. He wore blue jeans and weathered Timberlands.

"I know what you did."

I could feel the blood pumping in my chest as Matt Schroeder's icy glare focused on Nora, my dad, and me. Strands of yellow hair stuck out from the bandages on his head. Matt's voice was angry, and his pale blue eyes shifted between the three of us.

Nobody spoke.

Matt's voice shook with emotion as his eyes darted. "You killed my father. You killed my uncle. You tried to kill me. I saw you. I'm coming for you!" Matt was four inches shorter than my dad—and eighty pounds lighter—but he was strong-bodied and full of adrenaline. He looked so livid, it felt like he might attack us, but my dad's imposing stature probably discouraged him. I didn't feel very reassured, though. I was terrified of what I'd just heard.

Matt's yelling caught the attention of Detective Williams, who came back across the street. "Are you Matt Schroeder?"

Matt was breathing hard like he'd just run the Twin Cities Marathon. "Yeah."

"Could you come with me? We were planning to come see you at the hospital so we could take your statement. I'm surprised they released you so soon." Detective Williams looked concerned.

"It's them you should be tal—" Then he just stopped. He glowered at me, Nora, and my dad.

Detective Williams closed the distance between himself and Matt, gently turning him by the arm. They started to walk away together, but Matt separated and took off down the street, casting one final, furtive scowl at us before he disappeared from view.

My dad spoke, with an edge. "Come on, kids. We need to go right now."

I was so confused. And infuriated. I'd had a weird dream last night, but I would remember it if I left the house. It couldn't have been me. Right? Matt Schroeder seemed to think so. It was dark last night. How would he know? But *everyone* was acting weird. Detective Williams seemed to think it could be me. Did my own dad even think it could be true? The lawyer probably would too. I hoped Nora could see me—really see me.

Everything moved fast after that. We walked Nora to her place to make sure Matt didn't follow or pose a threat. Then my dad and I went home.

As soon as we got in the door, my said, "Pack your bag for Red Gut, gwis."

"We're going now?"

"I want to be ready to go at a moment's notice." He seemed nervous. I had never seen him like this before.

It was Saturday and we spent the afternoon packing bags and cleaning the house. My mom had been the disciplinarian when it came to chores at home. I scrubbed the toilet with one hand and used a rag rather than the broom to clean the bathroom floor. I stuffed long underwear, extra socks, and sweatshirts into my duffle bag with my other clothes. I grabbed some books too—*Attack on Titan, Volume 1*, *The Chalice of the Gods*, *Firekeeper's Daughter*. My dad loaded up the Subaru.

"Gwis," he said, his voice a little calmer now, "I just got an email from your school. They're canceling the last two days before break because of what happened to the Schroeders. The police want to take statements from everyone at the school. I called about an appointment for us with Detective Williams and they agreed that we can do it by Zoom from Red Gut. Let's go . . . we are hitting the road."

Red Gut

Chapter 6

IT USUALLY TOOK five hours to reach the Canadian border and almost another hour to make it to Red Gut Bay of Rainy Lake from there. My dad was a good driver, and the Subaru hugged the road no matter the weather. I slid into the passenger seat, threw my jacket in the back, and flipped up the hood of my Timberwolves sweatshirt. Then I texted Nora and popped in my Air-Pods. I scrolled TikTok for a while then put on J. Cole to zone out.

My dad let me be. His arm muscles seemed to involuntarily flex through his Under Armour shirt whenever he was turning. The steering wheel always looked so small in his Sasquatch hands. I started to relax as the city lights disappeared from the rearview mirror.

The topography in Minnesota gets better and better the farther north you go. The Twin Cities were built where the Mississippi River and Minnesota River meet. It was the edge of the Plains—open country, with cottonwood, ash, oak, and poplar along the wetlands and rivers. But now it was all pavement and rectangular buildings, shrouded in the ever-present dirty snow. Some of the bike paths and parks still gave a sense of the former splendor of the land itself.

I started to feel better just an hour north of the Cities. Here, the hardwoods started—maple, oak, and basswood. There were a lot of farm fields where trees had been cleared away for generations now, but they were still ringed by the hardwoods, and if people ever left the land alone there was no doubt the trees would reclaim the fields. It was prettier here, especially in autumn. It was clean and open. But there were still too many roads and people, parades of trucks and cars carrying cargo and people to and from the Cities.

My dad often shared stories about famous battles between the Ojibwe and Dakota in these parts, and great leaders like Hole in the Day, Sun Shining Through, Great Marten, and Flat Mouth who fought the wars, signed treaties, and kept land for our people on all of the ten largest lakes in Minnesota. I thought about all they had accomplished when we passed Fort Ripley, Hole in the Day Drive, Gull Lake, and some of the other places. I made my good hand into a tight fist and imagined what it would have been like to defend this land with a war club. We really should still have all of it.

North of Brainerd, the hardwoods start giving way to more pine forests—jack pine, red pine, white pine. There was more tamarack in the wetlands. There were a lot more grouse, rabbits, deer, and coyotes here, too. And more of us Natives.

We stopped in Walker, a town on the Leech Lake Reservation named after one of the white timber barons who made his millions exploiting forest resources at our expense. Usually on our trips up, my dad would talk about Roger Jourdain, who was tribal chairman at Red Lake— the rez next to Leech Lake—for thirty-two years in a row. He always had one of his family members or tribal employees drive him when he took trips to the Twin Cities airport, and he always made them stop in Walker.

"Get out," Jourdain would tell his driver. "Look. What do you see?" The marina there was full of sail and motorboats. Beautiful resorts and high-end homes lined the rugged shoreline.

His drivers usually responded nervously to Jourdain's gruffness. "Pretty boats? Pretty houses?"

"No," Jourdain would say. "I see white people. There are white people everywhere here. And you are on the Leech Lake Reservation right here. This is a Native American reservation, but white people own all but four percent of it. For generations, they have been coming after our land and resources. And they'll never stop coming. Our rez at Red Lake doesn't look like this, because on our rez, Natives own one hundred percent of the land. But they're coming for us too. And we will always need warriors who are willing to fight. Only now, the fight isn't with bows and arrows. It's with lawyers, politicians, and professors. We need every kind of warrior today. Now get back in the car and drive me to the Cities."

My dad would smile with pride when he told me that story. What it meant to him said as much about my dad as it did about Jourdain.

But today we just went through the drive-through at Hardee's and gassed up the Subaru. I kept my AirPods in, lost in thought. I think my dad had his mind fixed on getting us to Red Gut as fast as possible.

Once we cleared Bemidji, there were more animals than people for the rest of the trip. Here the timber wolves culled the coyote population and ruled the woods. I realized I was finally breathing normally as the sun set and the moon rose and the knot in my stomach from all the drama in the Cities had almost disappeared.

It took us about five minutes to drive through International Falls and even less to get waved through customs and immigration to cross into Canada. The big buildings there were cloaked in darkness, but I knew the mill was spilling toxic chemicals into the Rainy River and venting it into the air. The thought always made me sick and the smell just made me mad. In 2013, Packaging Corporation of America had bought the paper and pulp mill from Boise Cascade, but it didn't change much. Those were our waters they polluted, our fish that that they filled with mercury, and our forests they cut down and profited from. Lumber and pulp mills were evil in more ways than one.

A few minutes later we had pushed through Fort Frances on the Canadian side of the border. We had to pass through the Couchiching First Nation next. Canada agreed to quit calling our nations Reserves and switched to First Nations shortly before I was born, but their treatment of us wasn't any better than America treated Natives. We had some cousins at Couchiching, but visiting them could wait. We were related to most of the Dubois family there—and especially close with Elroy and Dora. They were second cousins, but my Grandpa Liam often took them fishing with us too.

We rolled across the Noden Causeway, which gave a spectacular view of Rainy Lake on both sides. Eleven thousand years ago, the glaciers here had scraped all the topsoil for miles around and dropped it on the Plains in Minnesota. The bare rock was often called the Canadian Shield. It was covered in deep lakes and scrubby jack pine, balsam, and black spruce. This was the heart of the boreal forest. The moon and stars were unimpeded by city lights and reflected off the pure white snow, illuminating the iced-over lakes and woods.

I pulled out my AirPods when I saw the signs for Bear Pass, Finger Point, and Wreck Point. Old Station Road on the left and Pair-A-Dice Road on the right marked our imminent arrival.

The actual Nigigoonsiminikaaning First Nation sign a little later was a monstruous blue appendage that seemed out of place along the pristine forest line. Grandpa Liam liked to joke that the sign started at the edge of the highway and ran through the ditch and woods all the way to their front yard.

As we turned onto the access road, I could see straight down the loop road to Swell Bay, the part of Rainy Lake where our community was, connected by water to Bear Pass and Red Gut Bay. The moon bathed the lake ice in luminescent light. There were two rows of houses, one on each side of the loop road that ran through the rez.

Nobody had yard lights on, but the shapes of houses and cars were clear in the glow of the moon, and a few of the houses had lights on inside. They looked so small compared to the trees, rocks, and lake. I felt a flutter in my stomach.

"We made it, gwis." They were the first words either of us had spoken in hours.

"Do you think they're awake?"

The Subaru rolled to a gentle stop in the driveway of the first house on the loop road. My grandparents lived in a small one-story house just a couple hundred yards from the access road. Most of the houses at Red Gut had no basements, in spite of the cold weather, because they were built on top of the Canadian Shield. It was rock all the way down. They'd just used cement pilings and built the houses on top of those, insulating all the walls, ceilings, and floors.

Grandpa Liam didn't have much of a lawn to mow in the summer either because the terrain was so rocky, but there was plenty of snow to shovel in the winter. There were trees and bushes growing out of every crevice in the rocks, though. In fact, there was only one lawn mower on the entire rez, and those ambitious enough to try and grow some grass took turns with the machine.

I could see my Grandpa Liam's old white Chevy Silverado parked in the driveway next to Grandma Emma's

Honda Pilot. I kicked open the car door and took a deep breath of the fresh, wintry air. It filled my nostrils, mouth, throat, and lungs. I just let my hands hang at my sides for a minute and closed my eyes. The cold never bothered me here.

My dad fished our bags out of the backseat and glanced at the house. My grandparents' house was painted sky blue, and in spite of being a small and humble affair, it was well kept. My Grandpa Liam was always tinkering and fixing things, keeping the paint fresh and the knives sharp. He built a screened-in porch on the house which he used to process animal hides during the cold months and as a sitting space in the summer. It had a commanding view of the bay.

The moonlight bounced off the snow in the yard well enough for us to navigate to the front door. Grandpa Liam and Grandma Emma never locked it, day or night. My dad gave the knob a turn and then the door one light heave with his shoulder. The door opened to soft, warm light from the kitchen of my grandparents' home.

Grandpa Liam was standing in front of us in long underwear, smiling from ear to ear. My grandpa was my dad's dad, but he looked nothing like him. Lean and wiry, but strong, he probably weighed about one hundred and forty-five pounds. He was short and dark brown, with wispy white hair that he kept long in spite of its sparseness. He looked a lot like a lean version of Pat Morita when he played Mr. Miyagi in the original *Karate Kid.*

Grandpa Liam was a man of the woods, practiced in the science, art, and culture of the Ojibwe harvest. In fact, I don't think he once had a regular job that paid a salary or hourly wage. He seined minnows and harvested leeches and sold them for fish bait in the summers. He picked pinecones, which sounds ridiculous, but he made over $7,000 every year doing that. He sold the pinecones to the provincial forestry program. They grew them into seedlings and used them to replant forest clear-cuts. And in the winter, he ran a major trapline. Grandpa Liam was seventy-four years old, but he was in better shape than most men my dad's age.

I had only spent long stretches of time at Red Gut in the summer, so fishing and leeching were familiar to me. But I'd always wanted to harvest my first deer or moose with my grandpa, and what I wished most of all was to learn about trapping. That's where Grandpa Liam made most of his money. But he also spent months in the woods in the winter, and that's what sounded best of all. We had a cabin in our First Nation's treaty lands at Chief's Ridge. Natives were the only humans who had used that land since the beginning of time. My grandparents even raised my dad on that trapline until my dad started high school. Whenever I told Noah, Oliver, Amelia, or my other school friends that my dad was raised on a trapline, they couldn't understand why. I couldn't understand why they left. *I'll get better answers to those questions on this trip*, I thought.

"Gwis," Grandpa Liam said, and folded my dad into a tight embrace. He turned to me next. "Ezra." He gave me a quick hug and then patted one leathery hand on my cheek, looking down at my cast. "You'll need a better injury than that to avoid chores around here, kiddo." I couldn't tell if he meant it or not, but he was smiling with genuine mirth, and the leathery crow's-feet by his eyes showed kindness and just a little bit of concern.

Grandma Emma was right behind Grandpa Liam in soft cotton pajamas with patterned roses. She wrapped my dad into a tight bear hug.

"Byron!" She kissed him on each cheek before he could even get his coat or shoes off.

"You didn't have to wait up for us, Mom."

"I was too excited to sleep right away, dear. Where's Ezra?"

Grandpa Liam moved aside and I stepped into the kitchen and Grandma Emma's fleshy arms. She kissed me on each cheek too. She smelled faintly of cedar. "How's your arm, Ez?"

"It hurts a little."

"Well, home-cooked food will charge your immune system and help you heal up in no time."

My dad looked a lot more like his mom, who was big-boned, tall, and broad in the face with long, strong fingers. Grandma Emma was a couple inches taller than Liam and probably outweighed him by twenty pounds. They looked like an odd match at first glance, but that was just the stereotypes talking. My grandparents had been married for over fifty years and they were still laughing all the time and holding hands when they watched television.

I stashed my coat by the door and kicked off my shoes. Grandpa Liam and Grandma Emma only had two bedrooms in their house. My dad took the spare room, and I usually slept on the couch with Buster, Grandpa Liam's dog.

"Mino-bawaajigen!" Grandma Emma smiled at me as she and Grandpa Liam went back to bed. It was never "goodnight" with them, just "dream well," since it was in our dreams that the spirits told us what to do with our lives. I smiled back at them and got into some sleeping clothes and settled in. It was only after a few moments that I heard a little bark and felt a small thump on the blanket.

Naming the dog Buster made most people smile because the animal weighed about five pounds. He was a mutt, and might have been a viable candidate for world's ugliest dog if Grandpa Liam ever bothered to take pictures and enter him in a contest. His fur was light brown, dark brown, and gray. He had an under-bite that showed his bottom teeth all the time. But he did have these big brown eyes that always seemed both smart and kind. He was a bossy cuddler, but I slept with my hand on his back every night, and Buster loved me for that—even tonight with my removable cast.

I also liked the couch because I could watch television every night if I didn't turn it up too loud. Tonight the Canadian news kept going on about a new disease in Brazil. I watched for a bit because new disease patterns were in the homework assignment from Mr. Lukas. It seemed strange to think about a disease in Brazil mak-ing its way to Red Gut, but Covid had put the whole world on edge about things like that now. Humans really were like nits in Mother Earth's hair—a plague on the planet, and so hard to get rid of. But Mother Earth was still in charge. Maybe the disease would be her way of rebalancing things.

When I couldn't watch any more news, I found a channel that had reruns of Ultimate Fighting Champi-onship. I used to watch UFC all the time with my mom. She was a huge fan and would rent all the big matches for us. We even went to one a few years ago when it came to Minneapolis. The memory was fuzzy now, but watching the reruns felt soothing.

Luckily for me, one from the early 1990s came on. Royce Gracie was not just the best of his time, he was the best of *all* time. After he fought, it changed the sport. The only way anyone could win after that was *his* way. The winners weren't the fastest or the strongest— they were the ones with the best ground game. They mastered choke and submission holds. Even the best strikers and fastest MMA fighters succumbed to anyone who got close enough to hold on and force them to submit. If I was ever in a fight for my life, that's what I'd do.

Chapter 7

IN THE MORNING, I woke to the smell of sizzling bacon. I shuffled into the kitchen and saw Grandma Emma wasn't holding anything back. She had eggs, bacon, hashbrowns, and French toast going. She beamed smiles at me as I shuffled into the kitchen and gave her another hug.

"Good morning, Ezra. How's my favorite grandson?"

"Gram, I'm your only grandson."

She winked and turned back to the stove. She wore leather slippers, a plain blue skirt, Frybread Power tee shirt, and a blue calico apron. I sat at the table and waited. Grandpa Liam was working on hides in the screened-in porch, but a few minutes later, he came in with a bluster of clean, wintry air. He kissed Grandma Emma on the cheek and washed his hands before he glided into a chair next to me. He wore brown woolen pants today with red suspenders and a white tee shirt.

"Grandson, bacon is the second greatest invention the white people ever made. It is a gift to the whole world. We should always respect them for that no matter how awful they are." He grinned as he slapped my arm, which rippled pain down to my hand and fingers. It was feeling a lot better, but it would take a little while before I didn't need the removable cast anymore. I tried not to wince and gave him an amused glance instead.

"If bacon is the second greatest thing the white man ever invented, what's the greatest?"

"Butter."

I smiled.

Grandpa Liam bent over the table, now shoveling food from the platters onto his plate with reckless abandon, talking with equal gusto. "And look. Bacon—one of the white man's great gifts to the world—goes perfectly with one of our great gifts: wild rice. Bacon and wild rice. It's perfect. And butter goes perfectly with another one of our great gifts: maple syrup. What this means is that the Great Spirit is telling us there's hope. Someday, we will all get along. We just have to pay attention to the signs."

Grandpa Liam eyed his plate when he was finished, poured maple syrup over the entire thing, then sat up straight and grabbed his fork. He tossed a piece of bacon to Buster, who tried to gobble it up but started to choke. I couldn't stifle a chuckle but Buster wrangled the bacon shortly after. I was about ninety percent sure that Grandpa Liam was just joking about all of this. But only ninety percent. With my Grandpa Liam, you never could be sure.

My dad joined us in a flannel shirt and blue jeans as Grandma Emma finished piling up the food on the table, and we all dug in with unbridled enthusiasm. Grandma Emma seemed pleased to have more than two people to cook for. Grandpa seemed pleased to have someone else receive his jokes. I couldn't help thinking he was right about the butter and maple syrup, which melted and ran together across the top of my French toast in a savory swirl. It felt good to be back at Red Gut.

My dad loved speaking Ojibwe with my grandparents. It was his first language, after all. I could follow along for a lot of it because of my long summers here and my dad's constant efforts at home, but I couldn't catch it all, so they switched to English from time to time for my benefit.

"Gwis," my dad said as we finished. "Let's kick your grandma out of the kitchen and do the dishes." He said it playful, but held his hand up to silence Grandma's protest. "After that we have our Zoom interview with

Detective Williams. I scheduled us for the first available time so we don't have to have that hanging over us the entire break."

That put an instant damper on my mood. Grandma Emma didn't have a dishwasher, so I scrubbed with one hand while my dad rinsed and dried. It didn't take long. I kept wondering what the interview would be like. I was glad we were here, and Detective Williams was back in Minnesota. It might have been easy to cross the border, but it was still a border, and that might mean he didn't have jurisdiction anymore. Right?

My dad brought his laptop to the kitchen table and connected his ridiculous oversize keyboard so he could type in his password and get on the internet. My grandparents had gotten an internet connection a few years before to please my dad, who needed it to check his email when he was at Red Gut, but I had never seen them use it themselves.

While we got ourselves set up for the Zoom, my grandparents both donned winter coats, hats, and gloves. Their conversation dropped to whispers as they got ready to step outside, so I couldn't catch the words, but Grandpa Liam and Grandma Emma seemed suddenly disconsolate for a moment as they looked at each other. If that was real or imagined, I didn't quite know. After so many years together, they had to have seen hard things as well as beauty. Maybe they were just worried about me. They stepped outside so we'd have the house to ourselves.

My dad motioned to me with one of his paws, "Abin omaa, gwis."

I sat next to him.

"We are going to talk to our attorney first."

It didn't take long for Paul Taylor to join the Zoom. He was a handsome man, about forty years old, with a short but stylish haircut and a gray suit and tie. He was Ojibwe too, from St. Croix—one of the reservations in Wisconsin. He had a private law practice in the Twin Cities, and it was either very successful, or he was taking out a lot of loans, because his clothes and the office behind him looked expensive. He was friendly as he engaged my dad in meaningless chitchat for a few minutes.

"Byron, how was the rice harvest at Red Gut this autumn?"

"I didn't even get out myself. I was stuck in the classroom. But my cousins said it was a good year."

"The Wisconsin beds haven't been producing as much the past few years. They think it's climate change. But a little further north has been better. Leech Lake buys seventy-five thousand pounds green from tribal harvesters. White Earth does the same. And Bois Forte buys another forty thousand."

"It's been transformational. Buyers used to pay one US dollar for green rice just a couple years ago. They're paying $6 now. Some of my cousins can make $1,000 a day for two weeks in a row."

"It's enough to make me regret becoming a lawyer!" My dad chuckled. "Only for a few weeks in the fall."

The lawyer laughed in turn.

"It is hard work, and it takes skill and equipment. But it's a lot of money too. Who would have thought that wild rice harvesting would become a multi-million-dollar business?"

"Right."

With that done, Mr. Taylor cleared his throat and took a deep breath.

"Ezra, my name is Paul Taylor. I've been friends with your dad for over ten years. Today I'm going to represent you during the interview. Do you know what that means?"

"I think so."

He continued: "They are doing these interviews with a lot of the neighbors of the Schroeders and quite a few kids at school, especially if they had recent interactions with Matt. It's a formality. You're not under suspicion of doing anything wrong. If you were, we'd be at an American police station and they wouldn't have approved you going to Canada. I will share a little information with Detective Williams to help make it clear that you had nothing to do with the fire. But that doesn't mean that you're a person of interest."

The voice in my head was screaming, *Tell that to Matt Schroeder!* But I didn't say anything. I did wonder what Matt had told the investigators during his interview. Was he implicating me and my family, like he'd started to do the last time we saw him? I just wanted this whole thing to be over.

"I'm going to do some talking at the start of the interview. Then the detective will ask you questions. When he does, give honest answers but keep the answers short. If they ask questions that don't sound appropriate to me, I'll object."

"Okay." It was stressful enough answering questions in class with Mr. Lukas. I wasn't looking forward to this. We shut down the Zoom with Paul Taylor and then joined another one with Detective Williams. Mr. Taylor joined too. We all knew one another already. Even Mr. Taylor and Mr. Williams seemed to know each other from other cases.

Detective Williams was wearing a brown suit and tie. He seemed serious, but courteous.

Attorney Taylor began: "Detective Williams, we'd like to save you a little time by offering a few important pieces of information. After that, Ezra will be happy to answer your questions."

"All right. What do you have for me?"

"First of all, on the night of the fire, Ezra was home all night. He broke a bone in his hand and needed a cast and stitches. The incident had numerous witnesses. His medical records confirm this information as well. He went home right after seeing the doctor and never left his house."

Detective Williams interjected, "Ezra, is this correct?"

"Yes." I kept it short.

Attorney Taylor continued, "The pain from Ezra's injury was significant, and to help him sleep, he took one dose of Percocet before he went to bed. I have emailed you a copy of his prescription and a note from the doctor. Given Ezra's weight and the dosage he was prescribed, it would have been impossible for him to wake with enough energy to walk six blocks, fight people, start a fire, and hold the door to their house shut, locking them inside while it burned."

I felt relieved to hear that I couldn't have made it out of the house that night. It validated my own hope that the crazy dream I'd had about the wolves and the fire was indeed just a dream—albeit a remarkable coincidence. I hadn't hurt anyone.

But there was new context that I had never heard. Someone fought with the Schroeders? Someone else started the fire? Held the door shut while they burned to death . . . ? My head was swimming in the details. I needed to talk to Nora.

Detective Williams was speaking now. "Thank you for all of that, Mr. Taylor. I have some questions for Ezra now."

"Okay."

"Ezra, how would you characterize your relationship with Matt Schroeder?"

I shifted in my seat.

Mr. Taylor jumped in, "It's okay, Ezra. You can answer the question."

"Uh . . . not good."

"Not good, how?"

"He's a mean kid."

"Is it true that you had a fight with him?"

"No. I never touched him. He grabbed my friend, Nora. I hit a locker."

"And that's how you broke that bone in your hand?"

"Yes."

"But you wanted to hit him?"

Mr. Taylor jumped in again, "Don't answer that one, Ezra. You got the facts here, Mr. Williams. That's all you need."

"Did you ever hurt Matt Schroeder?"

"No."

"Did you ever go to his house?"

"No. Well . . . I knew where he lived. It's only six blocks away from us. But I never went inside or ever set foot on the property."

"Can you think of any reason why someone might think they saw you or someone you know on the property the night of the fire?"

"No." I wanted an answer to that question as much as the detective did.

"Would you mind slipping the removable cast off your left hand and showing me the palms of your hands?"

I slipped off the cast. My hand was still sore, but the swelling had gone down. My stitches were covered with a small pad and butterfly tape, but my palms were visible in front of the camera.

"Thanks, Ezra. Can you think of anyone who would hurt Matt, Mark, or Luke Schroeder?"

I thought that anyone who ever *met* them probably wanted to hurt them. But I couldn't say that. *Keep it short.*

"No."

"All right. That's all for now. I'll let you gentlemen know if we need to do any follow-up."

"Thank you," Mr. Taylor nodded at the camera. "Mr. Cloud, I'll be in touch."

"Thanks." My dad seemed calm but cordial.

"All right. Have a good day, everyone." Detective Williams left the Zoom.

My dad waved at Mr. Taylor, clicked out of the Zoom, and closed his computer. "Gwis, I need to talk to you about something else."

I realized that he and I had hardly spoken since I broke the bone in my hand, even though I'd barely been out of his sight. In all honesty, we hadn't spoken that much for months. He'd been trying. But my anger was like a dark cloud—it was hard to see each other through the murk.

"I need a break. Can we do it later, Dad?"

"Okay, later. Later today."

"Fine."

Chapter 8

I SLIPPED ON A pair of insulated muck boots, a gray goose-down puffer jacket, hat, and gloves. The air was cleaner up here, but colder too. It took my breath away for a minute. The sunlight was painfully bright and I waited for my eyes to adjust. Grandpa Liam was at the end of the driveway, shoveling snow.

"You ever read *The Adventures of Tom Sawyer,* Ezra?" he called.

He was smiling as I approached. How did that old man know about the great books of the western world, living out on a trapline most of his life?

"I hate that book."

He laughed. "Mine's better. In *The Adventures of Liam Cloud* they still do a lot of chores but it's never a trick."

"If you need my help, Grandpa, I'll do my best." I grimaced at the thought.

Grandpa Liam laughed again. "I'm just giving you a hard time. Go ahead and take your walk. If I put you to work now, Grandma Emma will never let me hear the end of it."

"I'm going to see if Nora made it to the rez yet."

"Oh . . . her. She's cute." Grandpa Liam beamed mirth at my discomfort and went back to his shoveling.

I walked down the access road toward Rita Kingfisher's place, hoping that Nora and Ruth George had arrived. But I couldn't help turning back to shout at Grandpa Liam, "It's not like that! She's just a friend!" How had he expected me to shovel snow with my left hand still in a cast anyways? I could still hear him shoveling as I strode out of view.

I recognized Ruth's Toyota Highlander in the driveway at Rita's. Rita's house had the same exact design as my grandparents' home, but hers was painted light yellow. It sometimes felt like the Easter Bunny had a field day painting rez houses at Red Gut. My stride lengthened a bit as I approached the driveway. I felt my phone buzz.

Nora was texting me: *Wait there, I'll be right out.*

She was still sporting her Toronto Maple Leafs hat when she emerged, along with mittens and a new bright blue jacket. She smiled. I made a mental note that if I ever needed to get her a gift, I'd have to get her a variety pack of Maple Leafs gear so she'd have every color for her favorite team.

I waited at the end of the driveway. Nora strode up and gave a quick hug.

"Ezra, let's walk and talk."

Nigigoonsiminikaaning First Nation had about sixty houses and one small community center which got used for everything from basketball games to funerals. We just stuck to the tract house road because the snow was so deep everywhere else.

"I just had my interview with the detective." I gave her the entire story of the interview, including the new details—the altercation outside and someone holding the door shut until the older Schroeders died from smoke and fire. I wanted to tell her about my dream, but I didn't want to sound crazy. Besides, the attorney was sure that I couldn't have left my house and had all the evidence to prove it.

"There's something bugging me too," I added, nonetheless. "Why do you think Matt Schroeder was fuming at me like I had something to do with it?"

"Maybe he wasn't fuming at you. He didn't use any names. He just said, 'Hey you.' There were three of us standing there, Ezra—maybe he was yelling at *me*."

"Or my dad. I had never thought about that until now . . ."

"Or maybe he was confused. He was helping his father and uncle run a meth lab, Ezra. There's probably more than a few things wrong with him. Plus, he's been through a major trauma. Things like that affect people's judgment. *And* he's a white guy. To some of them, all Natives look the same."

I felt a little better hearing Nora's reassurances. But I still wanted answers to all of our questions. There was no way to know what Matt told the cops when he talked to them, but if he told them he thought it was me, it should have come out during my interview with Detective Williams.

"Nora, I bet that whoever held the door shut at the Schroeder's had burns on their hands. That must be why Detective Williams asked me to show him my palms during the interview."

Nora took a deep breath. "Do you think Matt wants to hurt us? Do you think he'd come to Canada to look for us?"

I took a breath too. "I don't know."

The thought was terrifying. And it must have been even worse for Nora. I had my dad and my Grandpa Liam and all his knives and guns where I was staying. And Buster. Buster was too small to protect anyone, but he always let us know when someone was coming. Nora just had her mom and her Grandma Rita. Matt had been harassing her even before the fire.

"Ezra, Charlotte and Amelia texted me. It sounds like Matt was put in foster care with his aunt in Milwaukee."

In spite of the many reasons I had to detest Matt, I did feel sorry for him then, all of a sudden. He had lost his dad and uncle and house and now he had to move hundreds of miles from everyone and everything he knew. Maybe his new home would give him a new kind of life—a better one. But I still wanted to be sure he wasn't a threat to Nora or me.

Nora seemed to read my mind. "Maybe he would want to hurt one of us if he could, but he probably won't get the chance. It has to be more than 300 miles from Minneapolis to Milwaukee, and even more to get up here. I don't think he can touch us."

"Maybe you're right." Noah and Oliver had messaged me that they hadn't seen Matt around since the fire. I told Nora the same. I don't know if either of us succeeded in convincing ourselves or the other, but it was something at least.

We walked in silence for a couple minutes, listening to our boots crunch the packed snow on the loop road. Then I thought of something.

"Nora, if we can figure out who did this, maybe we can get the cops and Matt Schroeder to leave us alone, no matter where he lives."

"Unless if the person who did this is someone we care about." She gave me a meaningful look.

"I know my grandparents and my dad. I really think they'd rather die than kill a human. I just can't believe it was them."

Nora didn't look convinced.

"Knowledge is power, Nora." I felt hope surging inside of me. "If we know, we can protect ourselves and our families, no matter who did what. We can make the decisions together. If there's someone we want to turn in, we can turn them in. If there's someone we want to warn, we can warn them. If someone needs to be protected, we can protect them."

Nora still seemed uncomfortable with idea of us playing detective, but she just sighed and we finished the walk back to her place in silence. She gave me another quick hug at the end of the driveway, and then waved goodbye from the porch before ducking into her Grandma Rita's house. I mulled over all the possibilities the rest of the way to my grandparents' house. I just couldn't see my family hurting anyone. My dad was with me when the fire happened. My grandparents were in Canada. None of them had any motive. They were all peaceful people. It couldn't be them. Nora, Ruth, and Rita . . . I couldn't imagine any of them having any reason to be at the Schroeders' house, much less the desire or ability to hold the door shut to a burning building until people died.

I turned down the driveway to Grandpa Liam and Grandma Emma's. The driveway and path to the front door were meticulously shoveled. No snowplow, snowblower, or professional service could have improved on Grandpa Liam's work. Despite the residual throbbing in my hand I felt a little twinge of guilt.

Chapter 9

I STEPPED THROUGH the front door and kicked off my boots, inverting them on the boot rack so they'd dry inside and out over the heat register. Grandpa Liam was in the kitchen wearing blue Dickies pants with red suspenders and a white tee shirt, boiling Conibear traps in a huge kettle on the stove. My dad was sitting on the couch tapping away on his keyboard. I looked back at Grandpa Liam. It seemed strange to boil metal traps.

"Grandpa, what are you doing?"

"I boil all of my traps. When you buy them from a store, they smell like metal. A beaver can smell that, even under the water. And the metal can catch a little bit of light, even through the ice. A beaver can see that too. I boil them and let them dry slowly on their own. It reduces the smell of metal and coats them in a thin layer of rust so they aren't so visible. I get about forty percent more beaver per trap doing this."

"That's cool. I never would have thought of that." Then I sniffed the air, catching something. "Is that cedar in the water?"

"That makes them smell like the woods and water. But it spiritually cleans them too. Cedar is strong medicine. We harvest animals for food and hides, but taking the life of an animal is not something to be done lightly. We have rules for every part of trapping, and it starts with offering tobacco and cleansing our tools with medicine."

I wanted to know more.

"Grandpa Liam, I know I have to miss trapping season every year because of school, but you could still teach me some things when I'm here."

"I'll be happy to, Ez." Grandpa Liam was staring at me, smiling through his eyes. It felt like he could see right through me. "Trapping is a specialized skill. It's very physical. But it's spiritual in equal measure. And you have to know many things—about the woods, the water, the animals, and yourself. Our family has special knowledge of this. It's secret knowledge, passed on in our family for generations. It's sacred knowledge."

Part of me felt like he was a crazy old man being super dramatic. But I also felt my heartbeat quicken as I listened to him. Why hadn't he shared more information like this before? Why was he sharing it now? Grandpa Liam took a step closer, his white hair in an ethereal trail behind him. "Ezra, I think Byron wants to have a word with you." He winked and turned back to his boiling traps.

The kitchen and living room were one big rectangle with no doors or walls between them. My dad was still sitting on the couch. He looked up, folded his laptop, and tossed it on the couch. "Have a seat, gwis." He motioned to the armchair. I sat. I had avoided this conversation as long as I could.

My dad sat forward, his large shoulders squared and his hands folded between his knees. His face looked serious and concerned, but kind. He looked so much like my Grandma Emma—his body type, face shape, everything. But as his gaze focused on me, his eyes seemed closer to Grandpa Liam's. I softened a little as I met them.

"Gwis, you are my one and only child. And my wish for you is the wish that every father has for his kid. I want you to have a long, healthy, happy life."

Ah. So this was about the comment I made about killing myself. I wanted to tell him that was just something I said in a fit of rage, but the words caught in my throat. I stared at him.

"Son, I know that you've been having a hard time. This thing at the Schroeders' is stressful for all of us. But you haven't said much about that, or even before that . . . what you've been going through since your mom passed away." He paused to draw a deep breath and continued. "I know you want a break from Northeast. You probably want a break from me too." Well, he wasn't wrong about that.

I didn't say anything in response, but I didn't look away.

"First, I need to know that you won't actually try to hurt yourself. I need to hear you say that you won't."

I really didn't want to have to answer him. I looked down.

I saw my dad's hands clench in fists and his voice came out forcefully. "Son, I could notify the authorities, put you in a seventy-two-hour suicide watch hold, and send you to inpatient counseling after that. I don't *think* that's necessary. But I need to *know* that's not necessary."

The picture he painted sounded horrible. "It's not necessary," I growled back, looking up.

"Because . . ."

"Because I won't hurt myself," I answered, my eyes flashing in anger.

"Thank you." He seemed relieved in spite of my tone. He unclenched his fists and sighed. Then he looked at me and took another deep breath.

"After the holiday, I'm not sending you back to school in Northeast."

"What?"

"You heard me. You won't be going back to school after the break. I made arrangements for you finish out the school year by completing your work from Canada. You won't be homeschooled. Technically, you will still be a student at Northeast. They will have assignments for you and you'll have to do them from here, turn them in by email, and attend some Zoom meetings with Mr. Lukas, Mrs. Byrne, and other teachers. I'll be printing a stack of worksheets and assignments. We have a schedule arranged for you to complete them and turn them in."

My mind was racing. This was exactly what I had hoped for—to be out of Northeast, away from Matt Schroeder's neighborhood, away from the house my mom had shared with us and all its memories, everything. I *did* want this . . . except for one thing. I wouldn't see Nora for months. I hesitated. Finally, I managed a curt "Okay." I must have seemed less than thrilled.

"I'll have to go back to the house in Northeast and teach my classes at MCTC, but I'll be back at Red Gut some weekends."

I glanced at Grandpa Liam. He was pulling his traps from the massive pot and laying them on towels on the kitchen table. He pretended not to be paying attention, but I knew he was listening to every word.

"That's not all, gwis. You're not staying here either."

My head snapped back to my dad.

"You're going to take your assignments with you and go to Chief's Ridge. You're going run the trapline with Grandpa Liam this winter."

I whipped around to face Grandpa Liam. He turned slowly, a big smile spreading across his weathered brown face. My heart was bounding.

"This won't be a vacation, Ezra. I'm going to teach you the meaning of hard work."

"I grew up on the trapline. I can vouch for the work part," my dad added.

I didn't know if this was my dad's version of a juvenile detention center, a way to protect me from Northeast, or a real effort to teach me our ways. Maybe it was all of those things. But learning to trap with Grandpa Liam in the wilderness at Chief's Ridge was a dream come true.

Liam's mirth-filled eyes were focused on me. "We have a lot of preparation, Ezra. We go to Chief's Ridge in fourteen days. But you'll have to work with me here every morning until then, sore wrist or not."

"Okay. I'll do whatever you need."

Grandpa Liam strode over and patted me on the shoulder. "We'll start tomorrow morning."

My dad finished. "You'll be at Chief's Ridge with no cell phone service or computer access much of the time, but we'll have a schedule where I bring new assignments to you there, and once in a while, you'll come to Red Gut so you can talk to your teachers on Zoom from Grandma and Grandpa's house."

I really wanted to talk to Nora and share the big news, but last I'd seen her, she didn't seem too happy about my pressuring her to help solve the Schroeder murder. Now I'd be telling her she'd be alone in Northeast. It probably wouldn't feel as safe, even with Matt Schroeder in Milwaukee. And she'd be on her own trying to figure out the case.

"Dad, will you help look out for Nora while I'm gone?"

"Of course, my boy. I will. Your mom's friend, Barb Greene, works at the Boys & Girls Club in Northeast. I'll have her keep an eye out too."

I paused for a moment, contemplating everything that could go wrong while I was gone. And hearing Barb's name had flashed me back to a memory of her laughing with my mom in our kitchen about a batch of frybread they ruined when cooking for the Minneapolis American Indian Center community gathering. They tried to feed it to our neighbor's dog, and the dog had choked.

My dad cleared his throat. "It'll be okay, gwis. It really will be okay."

I hoped he was right.

I helped Grandma Emma make supper that night. She had me chopping carrots, onions, and celery for a venison stew. She had a pink shirt and blue dress on with one of her calico aprons. As I watched her long, leathery fingers work the knives on the potatoes, I wondered how many she must have peeled and cut in her lifetime.

"Ezra, did I ever tell you about when I knew that I wanted to marry your grandpa?"

"No."

"I was only fifteen years old. Your Grandpa Liam and I grew up together. Everyone on this rez knows each other. But we only noticed one another the way kids do. I could shoot a basketball over his head. He noticed that."

"I let her get a few shots in when we were kids so she wouldn't be discouraged from playing ball," Liam interjected.

Emma laughed. But her story seemed more believable. She was still taller than Grandpa Liam.

"When I was fifteen years old, our house caught on fire. The whole house was made out of wood. It even had cedar plank siding, so the fire spread fast. We all went running out of the house in the middle of the night only to realize that my little sister Shawna hadn't made it out. I was screaming and crying, trying to get back to the house to get her. But the fire was so hot and moving so fast, my parents had to hold me to stop me from getting burned up. Someone called the fire department. But they take a while to get to the rez. I was crying so hard . . . feeling so helpless. We were going to watch my sister burn up with the house. She was only ten years old."

Grandma Emma's voice trembled as she continued, "And then, out of nowhere, Liam sprinted past all of us with a big brown woolen blanket trailing behind him like a cape. Nobody could catch him to stop him. He ran right into that burning house. He only lived a few houses down from us, and half the rez was on the housing road by then. We all thought he was going to die with her, but then he jumped through the burning window with my sister thrown over his shoulder and that blanket over them both. They were rolling in the snow by the edge of the road before anyone could even say anything. He saved her life, Ezra. He saved my sister, when nobody else could. He showed us all that he's the bravest Native in the world. I knew I'd always be safe with him."

"Ezra," Liam interjected again, "there are easier ways to impress a girl. I suggest one of the easier ways."

We all had to laugh at that. Even Buster started to bark.

"Grandma, why haven't I heard that story before?"

"It's not a secret," she said. "Everyone on the rez knows. At least all the old people do."

"I want to know all the family stories."

She paused for minute, seemingly lost in thought as she stared out of the kitchen window. Her face looked serious. Then she shook her head and looked over at Grandpa Liam. Her smile was back.

My grandma added, "Liam. You weren't trying to impress me. You just knew you were the only hope for Shawna. You hardly noticed me after that until I was sixteen and you were in the Fort Frances Fur Trapping Days contest!"

"Honestly, I probably wasn't thinking of anyone the day of the fire. I wasn't even thinking. It was all instinct," my grandpa replied.

"Instinct indeed," Grandma Emma said. "And the heart of a timber wolf."

"What happened at the Fort Frances Fur Trapping Days?" I asked.

"A man has to guard his mysteries, grandson. Let's save that story for another day. I'm starving."

Grandpa Liam seemed especially animated throughout supper, sharing more stories about trapping and hunting at Chief's Ridge. It started to dawn on me that bringing me there might be a dream come true for him too.

I sat on the weathered brown sofa after supper, next to Grandpa Liam and Grandma Emma. My dad sat in the recliner and turned on the television. We watched the news for a few minutes and then, at Grandpa Liam's insistence, we watched *Billy Jack*. The movie was almost as old as my dad, but it was the first Hollywood movie that showed a Native beating up a white man. Grandpa Liam loved that.

In spite of the sour mood I had been sporting for months, I couldn't help but smile when he laughed through all the action scenes and war whooped when Billy Jack confronted the white men in the middle of the Santa Fe Indian Market square. Buster barked when Grandpa war whooped. Grandpa Liam held

Grandma Emma's hand for much of the movie too. I bet they'd watched that movie a hundred times over the years.

She never complained, but he never gave her a reason.

Chapter 10

"NOOZHISHENH!"

It was so dark that I couldn't even see my own hands. Grandpa Liam was standing over me by the couch. I wondered how many times he'd said that before I stirred. "Noozhishenh! Ezra! We got work to do."

My body complained but I refused to give it voice. I sat up just as he turned on the light. He was already dressed—blue jeans, suspenders, and flannel.

"Get dressed and meet me in the kitchen."

He had oatmeal with milk and maple syrup on the table. He smiled at my grogginess and joined me, eating his oats in big, hearty bites. "We'll be prepping gear and packing first. And we need to take you shopping too.

The clothes you use for playing in the snow won't cut it at Chief's Ridge."

We started inside. He had a box full of knives. There were long fish-fillet knives, smaller curved skinning knives, rounded fleshing knives, and a variety of pliers and even garden shears and tree pruners. He laid out two sharpening stones and carefully demonstrated proper sharpening technique. Then he said: "Sharpen everything to a razor edge."

"Even the tree pruner?"

"Even the tree pruner."

"Why?"

"I use that for bone cutting on larger animals. It saves a lot of time not using a bone saw. If it's sharp, it's cleaner too. Wash everything up when you're done. Cold water."

"Cold water. Are you sure? Grandma Emma always makes us use warm water."

"Warm water is better for greasy dishes. But it can mess with the temper of the metal on cheaper blades and tree pruners. No more questions, now. Get to it." Then he winked.

I spent two hours sharpening every utensil with an edge that Grandpa Liam brought in from the porch or shed. He was being ridiculous, but I knew that he was trying to break me in so I didn't complain. When I was done, he said it was time to go shopping.

Grandpa Liam drove a white Chevy Silverado. The truck was older than I was, but Grandpa's constant tinkering kept it running fine. There was a little rust around the wheel wells from all the salt they dump on Canadian highways, to melt the snow off the roads, but it had four-wheel drive, good winter tires, and enough torque and traction to avoid most problems, haul his trailer, and get him to the trailhead for access to Chief's Ridge. I rode shotgun. In another year, I'd have a driver's license and all that freedom. I couldn't wait. Grandpa Liam had a folded blanket between us and put Buster on top of it.

"Why the blanket, Grandpa?"

"Buster is a fine beast. But he's pretty short, so he needs a boost so he can see." That old man loved his dog.

"Why does Buster need to see?"

"Just because Buster is a dog doesn't mean he doesn't have rights. Dogs have a right to see. Besides, if I ever drove in the ditch or got in a car accident, Buster would be able to run back to the rez or the nearest town and get help. He can only do that if he knows where he is. You gotta watch more TV, kid. Dog is man's best friend."

That made perfect sense to me. I guess dogs did have a right to see.

We drove back to Couchiching and across the Noden Causeway to Fort Frances. Grandpa drove about ten miles below the speed limit the whole way. He seemed intent on using every second not spent doing physical labor expanding my education about life. Some of his lectures were familiar by now, but a bunch today were new.

"Slower is faster, boy. If I drove over the speed limit, it could cost us hours in the ditch. Or the cops might give us a hard time. The Royal Canadian Mounted Police aren't much better than the cops in America. So, I don't give the RCMP any reasons to pull me over."

That made sense too. But everything that made sense also seemed a little ridiculous. I called that the Grandpa Liam Paradox.

We went to Fleet. Fleet stocked everything a Canadian needed—guns, ammunition, ice fishing supplies, camping gear, farm supplies, automotive parts, and winter clothes. "Stay, Buster," Grandpa commanded, and we strode into the store. I looked back over my shoulder to see the dog still perched on his blanket, craning his neck to eye the people in the parking lot.

Grandpa Liam made me push the cart as he thoroughly inspected every item on his list before tossing it in. He got food processing bags, burlap sacks, a box of nails, two large rolls of wire, and four sets of gloves—two with rubber coating and insulation for cleaning animals, and two with heavy layered lining for extreme cold. He got me three sets of long underwear and multiple layers of cold weather clothes, a winter facemask, hat, and two new jackets. One had a camouflage fleece overlay and the other was a black, shiny nylon puffer coat.

"Won't that make a lot of noise in the woods, Grandpa?"

"Indeed it will. You have the camo one to keep you quiet when I take you moose hunting. You have the other one for trapping. Animals are far smarter and more observant than people realize. If you are setting a trap in the brush and wearing that fleece, little fibers from the coat will catch on the brush. A fox will see those fibers and the broken twigs and you won't catch him. That shiny coat will slip across the brush without a trace, and you'll make more kills."

Grandpa Liam seemed to know everything about the woods. He knew his way around Fleet, too, even though town wasn't his natural environment. I felt awkward when we checked out. Grandpa Liam didn't have a credit card. He paid for everything with cash, carefully counting out the bills and coins. It made me wonder how he and Grandma Emma managed money in retirement. I didn't know the details, but I think my dad had health insurance and a retirement savings plan through Minneapolis Community & Technical College and he'd probably live off that when he retired. But Grandma Emma worked as an accountant for the Nigigoonsiminikaaning First Nation tribal office, and that was a part-time job. She probably didn't have a retirement plan. And Grandpa Liam made good money trapping, but they didn't have retirement plans for that. If he saved any, it was probably in crates in his shed. I never heard of him going to a bank.

"Noozhishenh! Grandson!"

I must have been daydreaming at the checkout.

"Grab your loot and take it to the truck."

I grabbed the big plastic shopping bags and we tied the tops shut and threw them in the back. Buster was still sitting on his blanket in the cab, carefully watching everything and everyone in the parking lot. Grandpa Liam rubbed Buster's head when he climbed in, pulled a stick of beef jerky from his coat pocket, and snapped it into three pieces. He popped one in his mouth and handed one to me and the other to Buster, who seemed to relish his with a special sense of importance.

Grandpa kept me busy for the next two weeks. He had a load of seasoned oak bolts dropped off at the house. He showed me how to run the chainsaw, and we took turns sawing and splitting the wood by hand with an ax and a splitting maul. My wrist ached every time I hoisted that splitting maul, but since the doctor never said I couldn't do it, Grandpa Liam had no pity for my complaints. Every muscle in my body was sore for the first three days too. But the job was done in five, and by then my body had gotten used to the effort.

"Ezra, if you keep working like this, you'll look like Arnold Schwarzenegger."

"Who is that?"

Grandpa Liam laughed. "Kids these days don't know anything. He's just an old white guy with muscles."

"I don't want to look old or white."

He laughed again. "If you get the muscles, you can walk by Rita's with your shirt off in the summer and see if Nora notices."

That was a pleasant thought. But then I saw Grandpa Liam still laughing at me.

When it was time, Grandma Emma cut my stitches and pulled them out with needle-nose pliers. It didn't even hurt. I'd have a scar, but my recovery from the injury was nearly complete. Grandpa Liam's two-week training program had produced the desired effect. We had just a couple of days before it was time to go to Chief's Ridge.

My dad stayed busy working on his computer during most of the past two weeks. But he joined us for some activities. And Grandma Emma made sure we all had supper together every night.

Chapter 11

CHRISTMAS WAS JUST ANOTHER chore day for Grandpa Liam. We never had a Christmas tree or presents like so many of the other kids in Canada and America. But I never felt like I was missing out.

Grandma Emma fried venison loins and laid them across a salad of mixed greens and vegetables. We watched *Dance Me Outside* again, or, perhaps I should say, we watched Grandpa Liam watch *Dance Me Outside* again. There's a scene in the movie when the young Native men are trying to distract a white man with made-up Native ceremonies, including telling him to choose his own spirit guide. The white guy stands up and screams, "Wolverine!" Grandpa Liam laughed so hard he could hardly catch his breath, slapping his knees and sending

Buster into a frenzy. Even my dad was laughing too, and it was a sight because he'd been so stressed. His big shoulders heaved and his voice broke from a baritone timbre to a high-pitched howl as he watched Grandpa Liam and Buster make a scene, drowning out the sound of the television with their hoots, howls, and giggles. Even Grandma Emma couldn't hold it in. I tried to stifle my own chuckle, determined not to let my dad see me enjoy myself, but Grandpa's laughter was contagious. I knew I had presents for Christmas, just not the kind that come in boxes.

I didn't get gifts wrapped in paper for my birthday either. My birthday was in July, but my mom used to make whoever had a birthday use that day to give presents to the people who brought them into the world—and the people who made their lives better. So, on my birthday, I usually made or bought presents for my parents and grandparents as a thank you. Sometimes I got something for Nora. This summer would be my second birthday without Mom. Thinking about that stifled my mirth at Buster, Grandma, Grandpa, and Dad.

My dad made a trip to Fort Frances the next morning to buy groceries for the house and trapline. Grandpa Liam had a long, carefully ledgered list of the food supplies to send with him as well as an envelope with cash.

My dad tried to protest, and offered to at least pay for my share of the food, but Grandpa Liam wouldn't hear it.

Grandma Emma had just cleaned the kitchen and sat in the recliner with a magazine when my dad left the cabin. As soon as the door shut, Grandpa Liam leaned over the kitchen table and whispered to me, "You gotta get lost for two hours."

"What?"

"You heard me. Go see Nora or take a walk or something."

He had done nothing but fill every second of my time with chores the past two weeks. I had no idea why this strange change of direction.

"Look, Ezra. All you need to know is that Grandma and I need the house to ourselves for the next two hours." He looked into my eyes, raised one white, wispy eyebrow, and made a dramatic pause.

"Grandpa, you're gross!" I exclaimed when things finally clicked.

"You'll think differently when you're my age, boy." He chuckled and slapped me on the shoulder. I hastily donned my coat, muck boots, hat, and gloves and bolted from the house.

The frigid air amplified the sound of my pants and coat swishing as I walked. I marveled at the animals who never had a respite from the temperatures, but still were able to survive out here.

I walked up to Rita's yellow house and knocked. Ruth answered the door, wearing black polyester pants and a light blue tee shirt. "Ezra, it's nice to see you. Come on in." I kicked off my boots and she motioned to the kitchen table.

The floorplan for Rita's house was identical to Grandpa and Grandma's. Rita had one bedroom and Nora and Ruth shared the other one. The house was uncluttered and immaculate; they didn't have all the tools and equipment that my grandparents had. Rita had made the large rug in her living room—a massive oval—faded slightly from years of use but unfrayed. Sometimes she sold her weavings for extra money. A large, beaded bandolier bag dominated the living room wall. Rita and Nora had beaded it together off and on for three years. It was cozy and comfortable there, although Rita kept the heat cranked up higher than I was accustomed. As I sat down, Ruth gently slid a pan of bannock bread on the table with her oven mitts, along with a plate and a butter dish.

"Miigwech," I murmered.

Rita beamed. "You're such a polite young man, Ezra. Come eat our bannock anytime."

"I'll be right out," Nora's voice came from the bathroom.

I could see two looms with fresh beadwork in progress on the counter. Both had floral designs, but one had flowers and vines in metallic hues—copper, silver, and gold. The other had classic woodland colors—green, red, blue, and yellow. The work was incredible. "Nora and my mom are working on new belts for their jingle dresses," Ruth offered.

"The beadwork is beautiful," I replied.

Rita wore a rose-colored blouse and blue jeans. She sat with Ruth and me at the table and started a long conversation about inverted polar vortexes. I didn't feel like I had much to say about that, so I focused on the bread and threw in some nods, downing a couple pieces before Nora emerged with a shy smile, already wearing her blue puffer coat and mittens with a backpack slung over her left shoulder.

"Let's walk, Ezra."

I thanked Ruth for the bread and slipped my winter gear back on. It was just Nora and me again, finally. Grandpa Liam's chore routine had really eaten into our chances to visit.

I decided to launch right into it: "Nora, I have some news. I'm not going back to Northeast. I'm going to work the trapline this winter with Grandpa Liam."

Nora gave me a meaningful glance, but her eyes were bright and her chin held high.

"I know. Your grandpa is so happy that he's been telling everyone on the rez."

I had to smile. Of course he had.

"I've always wanted to learn how to trap. And you know how much I hate Northeast. I know we talked about it, but I just feel bad that I won't be there to help figure out what happened or to be there if Matt, you know . . ."

Nora interrupted. "He won't be coming after us, Ezra. I've been talking it over with my mom and grandma too. He has to deal with a foster care placement in Milwaukee, new parents, a new school. Besides, I can protect myself."

"I know you can. It's not that. I just don't want to leave you alone with all of it . . ."

"That's sweet, Ezra." Nora smiled as she glanced at me.

I blushed and felt grateful that we were outside and walking side-by-side. Maybe she couldn't tell with the cold wind whipping at my cheeks.

"Ez, Matt could even be in trouble with the law. They had a *meth* lab at their house."

"Yeah. But he's a kid. And besides, all the evidence probably burned up in the fire."

"Okay, how about this: I'll make a deal with you. When I go back to Northeast, I'll keep my eyes open for any signs of Matt but still do what I can to keep looking for clues. I'll be careful so nobody knows what I'm doing. But I'll write down everything I see in a notebook. You do the same. Some of our clues might be up here on the rez too. We can prove that our families had nothing to do with it at least. We can even write down the things that don't seem like a clue. Maybe we'll see the patterns and connections later. When we see each other next, we can compare notes. We'll still solve this together. But my mom and Grandma Rita don't want me to talk to anyone about the investigation, so we'll have to keep everything a secret. Our secret . . . okay?"

"Okay." I blushed again. But I felt a little better at the same time.

Nora stopped walking and pulled the backpack off her shoulder, unzipping the main compartment. She pulled two red notebooks out and handed them both to me.

"I got these for our detective work. I figured you might not get to a store again before you go out to Chief's Ridge."

"Don't you need one of these?"

"I have a couple more for my notes. You get two too, in case you really do a lot of thinking. You're good at that." She smiled.

I gripped the notebooks and blushed yet again.

"Ezra, my dad died a long time ago. But I still feel like I missed out on a lot of things without him in my life. I don't even remember what he looked like. But I miss him. Or . . . I miss what he could have been. I keep a journal and write about it sometimes. I think it helps."

She looked directly at me then, and I didn't say anything. I just kicked a piece of ice down the road and watched the pine boughs swaying in the winter wind. So we started walking again, but I drifted just a little closer to her.

We walked the loop road through the housing tract and back to the shore of Rainy Lake. The ice was already fifteen inches thick and a few tribal members had used pickup trucks to plow a road across the ice toward Bear Pass. There were two fish houses closer to the village, each with a truck parked next to it. The muskellunge, northern pike, walleye, crappie, smallmouth bass, and perch fishing was usually great in December and January. The bay would have several more fish houses in the next couple of weeks.

"Nora, my grandparents kicked me out of the house for a couple hours so they could have alone time, to be romantic. I need to stay gone for a while longer."

She burst into laughter. "OMG, they are hilarious!"

"They're annoying, actually. They have a bedroom all to themselves every night! Why do they need the rest of the house?" But I was chuckling too.

"Well, Ezra, a true Casanova like your Grandpa Liam might need the bathroom, the living room, and the kitchen."

We were both laughing so hard we had to stop for a couple of minutes. Nora had to bend over and hold her belly. I put one hand on her shoulder.

We walked for two miles more down the ice road on Rainy Lake. Nora did most of the talking, but I was good with that. The bay narrows closer to Bear Pass and there are several islands there.

I caught a glimpse of movement ahead and tapped Nora on the shoulder. A white-tailed deer was trotting across the lake toward one of the islands. It was a doe, and she kept glancing over her shoulder behind her.

"Look!" I pointed my lips toward the shore of the mainland.

Two timber wolves were standing by the shore watching the deer. We didn't move. The deer was five hundred yards away and the wolves were a little farther than that. Then we saw three more wolves break from the tree line farther down the shore and start running toward the deer. The first two wolves suddenly bolted toward the other side of island. The deer started running, and all of them disappeared from our view.

"Did you see that?" I was excited. But Nora seemed little nervous. I guessed she had seen wolves before, but usually from the comfort of a car while driving.

"Yeah. I saw them," she replied. "Let's go back now."

We made it back to the village without incident, but as we walked off the ice and back onto the loop road, we heard a wolf howl, and then another, and then a chorus. They must have killed that deer on the island. It was almost two miles away, but it felt close.

We weren't the only ones to notice. The door to one of the fish houses popped open and we could see the silhouette of my namesake, Daniel Drumbeater. He spent as much time ice fishing as anyone else at Red Gut. He waved at us as he stood next to his fish house, staring toward the island and the woods beyond. We walked over to him and stood together for a minute. Silence returned to the woods.

"How's my namesake?" Daniel asked.

"I'm good."

"I'm glad to hear it. Don't worry about all that drama in Minneapolis." He swatted me on the shoulder. "You'll be safe on the rez." It felt good knowing that my namesake was looking out for me too, especially since he was the chief.

We left Daniel and walked past my grandpa and grandma's house so I could take Nora back to Rita's. She gave me a quick hug as we parted and I caught a subtle, faint aroma of perfume, for just a second. As I walked back home, I started to wonder why she would wear perfume on the rez. A sudden rush of heat rippled down my torso.

"She wears perfume for herself, not for me," I mused.

My dad's Subaru was back in the driveway when I got to the house. I slipped off my boots and turned them over on the drying rack, hung my coat, and looked for Grandpa Liam to see if he'd heard the wolves. The fire in the wood furnace was blazing, much hotter than normal, and I could see several candles on the table, recently extinguished. Grandma Emma was in the recliner thumbing through a catalog. I didn't know if I should sneak a picture of the candles to send to Nora for a laugh, or just run into the bathroom and take a shower to avoid the awkwardness of it all.

"Hi Ezra. How was your walk?" Grandma Emma was warm and welcoming.

"It was good. We saw timber wolves."

"Wow. That's cool. Where were they?"

"On the ice, close to Bear Pass."

"I'm sure your grandpa will want to hear all about that."

I heard voices coming from the screened-in porch where Grandpa Liam kept the trapping supplies. They were speaking in Ojibwe. I went a little closer.

"Gego agonwetawaaken! Gidaa-debweyenimaa. He's fifteen. He deserves to know, Dad." My dad's voice was earnest but not angry.

"I don't want him to know yet. I don't want to talk about it." My grandpa's voice seemed uncharacteristically tense. What could they be talking about?

"I love you too much to go behind your back on this. But it's a mistake. Ezra can handle the truth. If Ethan and Olivia were here, what do you think they would say?"

There was a long pause. My mind was racing. What kind of secret was this? Was it about the Schroeders? Or something else? Who were Ethan and Olivia? Why were the adults always keeping secrets from me?

"Maybe you're right. But not just yet. After his first kill."

"After his first kill," my dad agreed.

Grandma Emma put down her catalog and spoke much louder than she needed to. "Noozhishenh, go ahead and wash your hands. I'll have supper ready soon."

The conversation in the screened-in porch stopped and my dad slowly pushed the door open. I saw Grandpa Liam and my dad hold each other's eyes for a second more.

"What was that about?" I asked.

"Sorry, grandson." Grandpa Liam seemed a little sad. As curious and frustrated as I was, upsetting Grandpa Liam was the last thing I wanted to do. So I didn't press my question. Grandpa Liam seemed relieved and shifted into lighter conversation about the trapline. Grandma Emma started cooking a macaroni hotdish and fresh cornbread.

After supper, all four of us played cribbage. Grandpa Liam and Grandma Emma counted and pegged so fast I could barely follow everything they were doing. My dad just shook his head. He had cribbage skills too, but his fingers struggled to move the little pegs with any kind of grace. My dad and I lost every round to Grandpa and Grandma, but at least we didn't get skunked.

"Tomorrow is the day, noozhishenh. We're heading to Chief's Ridge. Get a good night's sleep. Just getting there is a job in itself."

Chapter 12

SLEEPING ENDED UP BEING a challenge. My thoughts were swirling—from the Schroeder fire, to the mysterious conversation I'd overheard, to Nora's perfume and the howling of wolves in the distance. It was so hard to know what was real and what was a dream.

Eventually, I did drift into a real slumber. I woke some hours later, but the house was completely dark. The sky outside was encased in thick clouds and there wasn't a hint of moon or starlight. Then I thought I heard something moving in the living room. Buster was still asleep, lying across my arm. I slipped my hand out from under him and slid off the couch onto the floor, leaving my bedroll on the couch. If there was someone or something in the living room, I was determined to see what it was this time.

I tried not to breathe too loudly or bump into anything as I slowly rose to my feet. All I could see was darkness. The furnace sometimes gave a faint glow around the edges of the wood loading door, but it must have been deep into the night, because the fire was nothing more than coals. Then I heard the sound of footsteps, light and agile. There was somebody there.

I reached for my smartphone on the couch armrest, planning to flip on the flashlight. But when I grabbed the phone the motion activated my screensaver. The light was faint, but it seemed overpowering compared to the darkness I'd been staring into. Then I saw, next to the bathroom door, a quick flash of brown and gray. My screensaver flipped off again before I could see more. What was it?

"Hey!" was all I could think to say.

There was a pause, then the bathroom light flicked on to reveal Grandpa Liam standing there in pajamas.

"Everything okay, noozhishenh?"

"Yeah, Grandpa. I thought I heard something in the house. Was . . . that you?"

The bathroom light was enough to illuminate the entire room now in faint yellow. But we were the only ones there.

"It's just me going to the bathroom, Ezra. Nothing to worry about."

The flash of brown and gray had seemed oddly familiar. In that moment, I felt a little bolder. "Grandpa Liam, have you ever been to our house in Minneapolis?"

"Why?"

"The way you move. It reminds me of something I saw at our house one time."

Grandpa Liam gave me a long look. He didn't look very tired, considering the hour. "I have."

I suddenly had a lot more questions now. *When? How? Why had I never seen him there? Why was that something to hide?*

But Grandpa Liam just said: "I love you, noozhishenh. Throw a few sticks of wood in the furnace before you go back to bed." And he went back in the bathroom and shut the door.

I reloaded the furnace and lay down on the couch. My smartphone said 3:37am. Well, I'd have that old man to myself for weeks on end at Chief's Ridge. I'd get all the answers there. I'd fill Nora's red notebooks, and I'd solve *all* the mysteries.

Flames licked at the wood in the furnace and the little house warmed up quickly. Buster was like a little furnace all by himself too. My body collapsed back into drowsy mulling and, finally, sleep.

Grandma Emma had every surface of the stove working magic at first light. Smoked beaver meat was tossed into the skillet with freshly browned bacon. She had pancakes and bowls of fresh fruit too. Grandpa Liam asked me and my dad to help him load the truck. He had a large trailer and drove the snow machine over the axles, affixing ratchet straps to anchor it in place. He had our crates of meticulously packaged and labeled supplies for us to put in the back of the truck. He had Duluth packs with gear and clothes. He handed an empty one to me.

"Load your bedroll into this, all the clothes and supplies we bought for you, and any other clothes you want with."

"What should I wear out there?"

"Go with layers. You'll have a long ride in the truck and then a long ride on the Ski-Doo. You don't want to be wet with sweat from having too much on in the truck. And you don't want too little for riding on the snow machine."

I was getting excited now. Grandma was done cooking by the time we had everything loaded. Grandpa Liam was full of stories about his best season on the trapline. Grandma Emma touched his cheek twice in the telling, and it occurred to me that she would really miss him while we were out there. They did this every year.

He would spend weeks on the trapline while she worked at the Nigigoonsiminikaaning First Nation tribal office. Obviously, their system worked for them, but it must have its downsides too.

My dad and I went outside with Buster and stood by the truck so Grandpa and Grandma could have a minute to themselves. Grandpa Liam came out soon after and the three of us got in the truck. My dad was going to drop Grandpa and me off at the snowmobile trail, then take the truck and trailer back to the rez before he went to Northeast Minneapolis for the start of the spring semester.

I sat in the middle with Buster on my lap. Grandma Emma stood on the front steps just a few yards from the truck and blew a kiss at us. As she waved goodbye, I couldn't believe that I'd never noticed before the distinct, discolored burn scar on the palm of her hand.

Chief's Ridge

Chapter 13

GRANDPA LIAM drove well below the speed limit toward the Dryden Highway, his black Carhartt suspenders buckled over a white woolen base layer from Fleet. His hand seemed relaxed on the wheel, but his eyes steadily scanned the tree line and ditch for any sign of moose or deer. A collision could be deadly, especially with so much ice on the road.

I sat in the middle with Buster. I'd tried to follow Grandpa Liam's advice with a base layer and fleece pullover, keeping my coat in my lap. But between the coat and Buster, I was sweating before we even got off the rez. My dad rode shotgun, ponderous hands folded in his lap, just wearing jeans and a green Lakehead University sweatshirt. He got a lot of university spirit wear when he gave talks if they had it in 4X. He was quiet too, lost in thought. I knew he was worried about me and I guess I hadn't reassured him much over the past year. I had been so immersed in my own feelings, it was easy to forget that this must have been a hard time for my dad. I spent much of the drive thinking about if and how to ask about the scar on the palm of Grandma Emma's hand.

Grandpa Liam was a welcome distraction for both of us. He was determined but in good spirits as he narrated the story of Adikokan.

"There's a place north of Chief's Ridge called Adikokan. Some French guy wrote it on a map as Atikokan and that's how it reads on Canadian maps today. It's a sacred place. Adikokan means 'Caribou Bone.' Our treaty lands used to have tens of thousands of woodland caribou. The caribou who survived our hunters and the wolves and lived to old age for caribou went to Adikokan to die at the end of their lives. There are thousands of caribou that died there over the years, all elders, wise in the ways of the woods. They outsmarted both people and wolves for years to live so long. The wolves respect this place. They won't hunt there. It's a refuge that all animals honor. So we honor it too.

"Many years ago, one of our people made a big mistake. He told a white anthropologist about Adikokan.

White people don't have honor the way we do. They don't respect the woods. They don't respect the sacred. The anthropologist published the story. That's what they do. I suppose he thought it made him look smart and special. White guys have whole academic disciplines devoted to getting information out of Indigenous people so we can be objects in their museums, literature, and academic publications. Anthropology is just one of those. The name of the Native man who shared the story didn't even go into the publication.

"The publication went in some obscure journal and only about twenty people ever read it. But one of the people to read it was another old white guy with a bunch of degrees. He was an archaeologist. His idea was to dig up Adikokan to see if the story was true. Some other old white guys from the Canadian government funded his dig, mainly because their political campaigns were paid by the big forestry companies. If the archaeologist got to dig up Adikokan, someone would have to build him a road and clear some trees. Then they could cut more trees and build more roads.

"They had been cutting near there since 1890, but after the dig, they cut it all. They clear-cut hundreds of kilometers of virgin pine forest around Adikokan. The archaeologist dug up the entire site. White hunters drove down the logging roads and shot the last surviving woodland caribou. There are only a few hundred left, on one of the Lake Superior islands on the other side of Thunder Bay.

"You know what that archaeologist found? Thousands of caribou skeletons. Acres of them. So he got to publish a paper and get tenure at a university. And white people in Canada got to sip coffee and talk about how neat it was that old caribou went to this one place to die a long time ago. In 1930, they built a mine there and polluted the whole area. There are two thousand white folks living in a town with the same name nearby.

"You know what we got? Destroyed resources. Violated treaty rights. Desecrated sacred sites. You know what the caribou got? Mass extinction. Roger Jourdain said it best: 'You can work with the white man. You can be friends with the white man. But you can never trust the white man.' He has no honor, no respect."

My dad shook his head as Grandpa finished. "It's enough to make you mad for another five hundred years."

I was upset about the desecration of Adikokan too, but I was amazed that the caribou had carried on this tradition for generations and that the wolves honored the place and hadn't hunted there. Animals were so much more than animals. There really was a law of the woods.

Grandpa Liam was done with story, but he added, "At least they didn't get our treaty lands. Ezra, I am taking you into the most pristine and abundant forest in the world. Only Natives would protect a place like this. It's a treasure. Just don't tell white people about it."

His Silverado slowed to a crawl as he turned off the highway. It rolled and bumped and heaved onto a logging road. The logging road was plowed for winter cutting, but describing it as rustic would be too kind.

"Time for your Red Gut massage, Ez." Grandpa winked as the road rocked and bumped us around in the cab.

"Are we going to Adikokan?" I asked. Grandpa Liam waited a long time to respond.

"No. It's still sacred. And we still honor the code. Adikokan is too far north and east anyways. We're done with the main highway already. It's faster to access Chief's Ridge from this side of the treaty lands. A few hours in the truck and an hour and a half on the Ski-Doo. We could get there by taking the snow machine through Bear Pass, across Rainy Lake, but we'd have eight hours on the machine to get there with all this gear. Unloaded, we could make that distance in five, so that's how we'll come back for breaks so you can have computer time."

There was a clearing by the logging trail and massive stacks of timber where the machines had skidded the logs out for loading. I knew we needed to cut wood for building houses and making toilet paper, but seeing the scale of the operation still seemed gross to me. Some things should be done in moderation, or not done at all.

"This is about as close as we can get with the truck." My dad's baritone pulled me out of my head. He tapped me on the arm as the Silverado lurched to a stop. My wrist was feeling much better. It throbbed once in a while, when I tried to lift or put pressure on it, so I still used the removable cast to make sure I didn't reinjure it.

Grandpa Liam's Ski-Doo was a newer Skandic. As far snow machines go, this was one of the biggest utility snowmobiles on the market. He had a hitch and connected a massive game sled. My dad and I carefully loaded all the gear into the sled with Grandpa Liam giving orders every step of the way. He was tough. He had done this solo for decades, and we had never heard him talk about quitting or slowing down. We used ratchet straps to cinch everything down.

Buster didn't mind the snow, but he was so tiny he couldn't go anywhere that wasn't plowed. I had fun watching him playfully flounder in the deep snow while we finished loading. When we were done, my dad tapped me on shoulder and gave me a hug. This was where we said goodbye. I didn't really feel like hugging him back, but I didn't push him away. He hugged me and then held my shoulders for a second after we separated, giving me a meaningful look. I knew there was more that he wanted to say, but perhaps it could wait.

Grandpa Liam straddled the seat on the Ski-Doo and motioned to Buster, so I scooped him up and handed him over. Grandpa Liam tucked Buster inside his coat so Buster's head stuck out right at the neckline.

"Dogs have the right to see," I said.

"Your boy is a quick learner, Byron," Grandpa Liam quipped.

I hopped on the back. It was stiff and awkward because we had our heaviest coats and bibs on. The air was cold, but cruising on the Ski-Doo would make the windchill serious. My dad watched and waved as we took off. After a little while I looked back, and his truck was already headed back to Red Gut.

Riding on the snow machine was slow and bumpy at first because there was no obvious trail. But once we made our way down to the Rainy Lake shore, Grandpa Liam opened it up. The wind started to needle through my coat and the sweat close to my body felt like a frigid towel, but I didn't complain. I wanted to see and smell everything. I felt free riding on the snowmobile—nothing but clean, clear snow, ice, and trees for miles around. The sunlight was brilliant across the winter landscape, making everything glint and glitter. It felt like we were cruising through fields and hills of diamonds. I wondered if we would see more wolves; if I would get to shoot my first moose; if Grandpa would show me his secrets.

Once we cleared the bay, we were back in the woods. There was a trail here, but we must have been the first people to use it this winter. The snow drifted and settled on the trail and we had to go slow, because any fallen trees could stop the Ski-Doo instantly and get us all killed. Twice I had to hop off the Ski-Doo and use an ax to clear fallen trees. Eventually, we started to ascend a series of hills, steeper and steeper until we came to a clearing on top of a large, rocky prominence with a view for miles in all directions, and saw a tiny log cabin nestled by the edge of the clearing among a stand of balsam.

Grandpa Liam gunned the Ski-Doo and pulled up right by the door. "Home," he said.

I slid off the Ski-Doo, awkward in my heavy clothes, and surveyed the landscape. The tree line had a mix of black spruce, balsam, birch, red pine, jack pine, and poplar. There was a clearing adjacent to the cabin, but I could tell there was a trail cut through the trees on each end of it. We were on high ground here, and through the bur oak and poplars south of the cabin was a steep hill and a lake. Everything was shrouded in drifting snow, without a human footprint for miles around, save the ones left by Grandpa Liam and myself.

It was perfect.

The door had no lock. "Grandpa, aren't you worried about people stealing your stuff when you're not here?" He laughed.

"First of all, Ezra, only Natives come here. It is taboo to steal in our culture. Someone who steals from you is giving you part of their life. Nobody would be stupid enough to do that. And if they did, it would be a gift to us. I'm seventy-four. Nobody has ever taken anything in all those years."

"Are there other trappers that use the cabin?"

"No. There are several professional trappers from Red Gut. But each of us has our own area. Morgan Greenleaf traps in Cherry Valley. Dustin Fairbanks works the Twin Lakes Flowage. Great beaver trapping in there. We have an ancestral claim here. It's tribal land, rather than personal property, but there's enough tribal land for everyone to have their own area within that and we all live the Ojibwe culture. That means respect."

He pushed open the door and fished Buster out of his coat, sending him in first. "Sic 'em!"

I must have looked confused.

"Buster is a good mouser. The mice are the only invaders here."

Grandpa started by building a fire in the little Drolet stove in the middle of the cabin, then quickly directed me to start unloading. It took me almost an hour to unload without any help, and Grandpa's super specific instructions about where everything needed to go. There was a storage shed just a few yards from the cabin and it was full of boxes, hide stretchers, traps, and tools. I carefully stacked the trapping supplies there along with cannisters of gasoline for the Ski-Doo and kerosene for the lamps. That was most of the cargo. I brought the rest in the cabin. Then he sent me outside again to find a snow shovel and clear a path from the house to the shed, shovel off the roof of the cabin, and bank snow around the outside of the cabin for extra insulation. Finally, I got to come in and really look around inside.

The cabin was small: eighteen feet by twenty, and all one room. There were two bunkbeds against one wall. There was a sink with a drain running through the wall, but no running water. There were pots and pans hanging too. The Drolet stove in the middle of the cabin was big enough to heat the entire space quickly, but it also had a flat top so it could be used for frying and cooking and a warming oven next to the main combustion chamber. There was a kitchen table with four chairs. But there were no couches and only one rocking chair, placed near the fire. There was one small window on each side of the house.

The biggest surprise of all was that the north wall of the cabin was covered in book shelves from floor to ceiling, and every shelf was loaded with books. I walked over and started to browse. Most were in English, and included famous titles that we had to read in school. There were books for every reading level; I even saw a section of fantasy books including George R.R. Martin, J.R.R. Tolkien, C.S. Lewis, J.K. Rowling, and Edgar Rice Burroughs. It was quite the library. There were also books in French, and a ton in Ojibwe, including works by Pat Ningewance, John Nichols, Rand Valentine, and Isadore Toulouse. Lots of people had been publishing in our tribal language, especially over the past twenty years.

"I guess I know where you read *The Adventures of Tom Sawyer* now."

Grandpa Liam smiled. He was full of surprises.

He had me fill the kerosene lanterns next and bring the food inside. Most of it was dried food, a few canned foods that wouldn't be good to freeze, and a couple perishables for the first few days.

"There are too many animals out there to risk our food supply being in the shed. It's January now, but by the end of February, they get pretty hungry and some take bigger risks, looking for food where the humans are. If you get a moose, we'll cut ice from the lake and skid it over here to the shed. I have a storage cache dug in the ground. We'll pack it with ice and sawdust. It would stay frozen without that, but the ice and sawdust insulate the smell and make it hard for the animals to get at it."

I went back outside to shovel a path to the outhouse and bring wood from the rick by the shed into the house. Then I filled several pots with snow to melt down and store for drinking and cooking water. When the sun set, Grandpa Liam cooked us pork chops on the Drolet with potatoes. My dad had sent a blaze-orange satellite phone powered by a cold weather battery in case of emergencies. I pushed that up against the west wall out of the way, behind the fox stretchers.

After supper we brushed our teeth and I settled on the lower bunk of one of the bunkbeds. I sorted out my bedroll, stripped down to my long johns and base layer shirt, and climbed in. Buster joined me without hesitation. Grandpa Liam brought over one of the kerosene lanterns and grabbed a book off the shelf. It was called *Awesiinyensag*, and was written entirely in Ojibwe.

There were stories in there by Nancy Jones, Eugene Stillday, Anna Gibbs, Marlene Stately, and Rose Tainter. He sat on the edge of my bed and started to read out loud.

A little voice in me said the story Grandpa really should be telling me about was the scar on Grandma Emma's hand. But it felt wrong to bring up now. I just had to find the right time to ask. I was also thinking that I was fifteen years old: I wasn't a little kid who needed someone to read to him. But I didn't stop him.

I thought about the deep snow piled up around the cabin, drifting in the winter wind. There were only five people on planet earth who knew I was here, and they weren't telling anyone. I thought about the animals in the woods: the minks and beavers we'd try to trap, the deer and moose navigating the deep snow, and the wolves in constant pursuit. I listened, to my grandfather's aging, tenor voice, the wind swirling around the cabin walls, and Buster's easy breathing next to my body. Grandpa Liam reached one calloused, veiny, wrinkled hand out and gently stroked the hair from my forehead to the pillow. I drifted off into deep and unencumbered sleep.

Chapter 14

I WOKE with an involuntary shiver. The cabin was cold and Grandpa Liam was just stoking the remaining coals in the stove. He was already dressed in SOREL boots and Thinsulate bibs over his base layer. The sky outside looked like slate: overcast, with just the tiniest hint of light.

"Big day today, grandson. We're going to set the line."

I rubbed my eyes and slipped on my boots to go out to the outhouse. I would have preferred to stand in the doorway and relieve myself, but Grandpa Liam said that people who pee by the house invite bad karma. Good luck, good energy, good spirits, and successful trapping and hunting required cleanliness. Good spirits are attracted to clean places, and bad ones hide under garbage and are attracted to bad smells.

We ate oatmeal at the table. Buster had killed three mice already. Grandpa gave him some dog food and patted him on the head. He took the mice outside and set them by a tree with tobacco.

We reloaded the sled with traps, snares, two axes, two hatchets, two knives, a chainsaw, mix gas and bar oil, wire, and rope. I put on the trapping coat Grandpa Liam got for me and my insulated boots.

He left Buster at the cabin. "He'll kill more mice when we're out of the cabin. And I wouldn't want to chance him getting into a snare or spreading his scent around my sets."

The trapline ran for miles. I was used to calculating the distance in miles, but Grandpa Liam used kilometers. "You'll have to honor your Canadian roots and do it my way, kid."

With that, our day really began. I never worked so hard in my life. There was a trail, but the snow was deep and it was slow going. He reminded me how to start the chainsaw—keep my left arm stiff, and let the saw cut through logs. All the practice I had on his piles back on the rez was helpful now. We had to clear several deadfalls with the saw and a few smaller ones with the ax.

Once we were on the main trail, Grandpa Liam stopped every forty or fifty yards, walking into the woods and making sets for fox, bobcat, and lynx with a snare or midsize Conibear trap. He talked me through the process but he made all the sets that day. Where there were denser stands of balsam and black spruce, he used the blunt end of a hatchet to tack marten sets against the trees.

There were several small lakes in a chain along the side of the south loop trail and here we worked on beaver sets. He made me chop holes in the ice with an ax, rather than cut a hole with the chainsaw, so the gas from the saw wouldn't discourage beavers from our sets. I had to cut saplings about eight feet long and wire two to each Conibear. He showed me where the beaver food stashes were located, under the ice, by the sticks coming through the ice some yards away from their lodges. It was a careful and precise effort to get the Conibears set right on the runways from the lodges to the food stashes. I could see the wisdom of boiling the traps now.

"The beaver is the heart of trapping, Ezra. They eat nothing but medicine—lily pad roots, willow saplings, poplar buds. They are what they eat. So the meat of a beaver is pure medicine. It's loaded with vitamin A and many others. This is one of the secrets to the longevity of our people before colonization. We got nutrients through the animals we ate, not just the berries, nuts, and vegetables we foraged for. Beaver is one of the healthiest foods on the planet. And beaver furs are one of the top money getters in our operation. Nobody has ever killed a beaver in his lodge. No human and no wolf. We always have to catch them outside of their lodges."

We worked all day long setting traps and snares, moving in a long loop. Whenever we set a snare, Grandpa Liam placed a long skinny stick in the snow about five feet high and peeled the bark off the top end of the stick.

"Why?"

"Some of the sets are set back from the trail a ways. When we check traps, you won't be able to see if you got something from the trail. But with this stick, if I don't see the peeled end of the stick standing there, I know I got one because the animal knocked it over. And if it's still there, I know I didn't. This will speed us up when we check snares and traps. Today we set the south loop. That's only half our set and it took us all of the daylight— ten hours. Tomorrow we set the north loop and it will take the same. When we check our sets, the trail will be cleared of deadfalls and the snow will be packed by the Ski-Doo and we can check both loops in just a few hours. The rest of the daylight on those days we'll spend cleaning animals, processing hides, and reading books."

I couldn't help but marvel at the genius of his woodsy knowledge.

When we finally got back, Buster was happy to see us. The cabin had enough residual heat to keep him warm, but the fire was out. Grandpa told me to build the fire this time and he cooked pork chops and eggs. I knew the eggs and pork chops wouldn't last long while we were out here, and I was famished.

Day two was almost identical to day one. The north loop was even more beautiful than the south. There was a much larger lake here and the north loop circled the entire lake. The far side of the lake had a huge cliff with white pine, jack pine, balsam, and spruce covering the top, except for a ridge jutting out by the lake on the highest point of land.

When we approached the lake, Grandpa Liam pulled the Skandic up by the shore and shut off the engine. "Come here, Ezra." The edges of Grandpa Liam's wrinkles caught the sunlight, making the furrows seem even darker by contrast. He held his chin high as he gestured at the landscape with his mittened hands.

"We call this lake Manidookaan. That means 'The Place of Spirits.' This lake is four kilometers across and six kilometers long. It's at the highest elevation in the entire watershed—closest to the sky. There really are spirits here, deep in the water, high in the sky, in the woods all around us. On clear nights the northern lights dance in the sky here. In our way, we see the northern lights as the souls of our ancestors. They dance with one another. There is no light pollution from cities and towns and houses here. It's the closest we can get to touching them."

He cleared his throat and looked at me. "You see, Ezra, when someone dies, they don't really die. It's just the body that dies and goes back to Mother Earth. The spirit is forever. So we never die. We just change worlds. And this place is where the two worlds meet. The world of the living and the world of the dead. There is nothing to be afraid of where the two worlds meet. Our dead relatives love us as much as we love them. They would never hurt us."

"Grandpa, have you ever seen someone after they changed worlds? Is that even possible?"

He gave me a long, earnest look and turned his gaze back to the lake and shoreline. "I have dreamed of people who changed worlds. Vivid dreams. But seeing them like we see each other today, that probably won't happen until I change worlds myself."

"I can't even dream about my mom. What if I forget what she looks like?" I looked down, feigning interest in my boots.

He put a mittened hand on the back of my neck. "You will dream of her again. And you'll never forget."

I had my doubts about the forgetting. But somehow, it felt reassuring to hear him say that and to think of changing worlds this way. I gazed at the lakeshore to the top of the escarpment.

"Does the north loop go all the way up there?"

Grandpa's response was confident and energized. I watched his lips move in the crispy air and his mittened hands gesture to the trailhead. He seemed so happy to be able to show all this to me, even proud.

"Our trapline goes behind the ridge a little farther away from the lake. We call this whole area Chief's Ridge, but that high point of land overlooking Manidoo-kaan? That is what gives this place its name. Chief's Ridge isn't called that because of a great chief or leader of humans. Can you think of why?"

"Is it because of a powerful spirit there?"

"Not exactly. It's because of the wolves."

"The wolves?"

"Yes. Since the end of the last ice age, over eleven thousand years ago, there have been wolves and Natives living here. But that ridge is owned by the wolves alone."

"We've been studying keystone species in class with Mr. Lukas."

"That's good, Ezra. That's part of the story."

"What's the rest of the story?"

"If you know about keystone species, you know that wolves give order to the entire ecosystem. How do they do that?"

I thought for a moment. "When they den in a certain area or hunt an area intensively, the deer, moose, and other large game animals leave so they can live. And that reduces the impact they have on the plants there and makes it possible for smaller animals and birds to flourish, because there is more food for them."

"That's right. And do you know how a wolf pack is organized?"

"I'm not sure. I know there's an alpha male and an alpha female, and they're in charge."

"That's right. There are many kinds of wolves. They mate for life and they are devoted to their partners. But the partners are also devoted to one another. They hunt together. And they raise the pups together. They are strong in a pack. The alpha male doesn't typically fight all the other male wolves to establish his dominance. He has the most pups and then works with his pack and leads his pack, but he has no special power without his pack. By understanding all of the members of his pack and loving them all, he keeps their unswerving loyalty. Wolves are far more loyal than humans by nature. So if the alpha says that they will den at that ridge, that's what they do. If he says that they hunt the Cherry Lake Valley for the next month, that's what they'll do."

Grandpa Liam's gaze was earnest. "We know these things because our ancestral knowledge has been passed on for millennia, just like I am passing it to you right now. We don't need white scientists or archaeologists to tell us. We have our own knowledge and our own ways of knowing. For eleven thousand years, an alpha timber wolf has made that ridge the center of the pack's territory. That's why we call it Chief's Ridge. The chief isn't a human. It's the alpha—the leader of the pack. He's more powerful than any human."

"Wow."

I thought about all the generations of wolves, each with a leader who called this place home. And I thought about all the generations of our people who called it home too. It was hard to describe, but in that moment I felt a connection to my own ancestors and the woods and wolves, more deeply than I ever had before.

"Grandpa, what about the omega? Isn't there a lone wolf? An omega."

"There is always an omega. The life of the lone wolf is the hardest of all the wolves. Most wolves live for ten years. Once in a great while, one lives as long as fifteen or seventeen, but ten is probably the average. A lone wolf can't successfully hunt big game. He has to scavenge,

→ 142 ←

hunt small game—even mice—and hope he can find enough to make it through the winters. They usually don't live as long. But the ones who do live a long time never live a long life by staying a lone wolf. They have a time as a lone wolf, sometimes a year or two, or even three, and that time makes them so strong and so cunning and so adaptable that they rejoin the pack. And not always—but sometimes when they do—they replace the alpha as leader of them all."

"That's so cool."

"You know, Ezra, we are wolf clan. We thrive best in a pack too. Which one are you now? The alpha, the beta, or the omega? And who will you be when you grow up?"

I hadn't really thought about that before.

"Just something to think about," Grandpa Liam said. "By the way, the alpha here now is a huge gray wolf. His coat is so light that he almost looks white, like an arctic wolf. I call him Ogimaa."

After that we finished our work for the day, setting traps and snares along the north loop road. When we got behind Chief's Ridge there was dense forest and Grandpa Liam set some fisher traps. Fishers are almost as big as an otter, but they were in the weasel family.

"The fisher is the most ferocious animal in the forest," Grandpa Liam laughed. "Ounce for ounce, they're the toughest. The fishers and bobcats are always at war with one another. They even kill each other's babies. The fishers are winning right now. And during the up cycle for them, we usually have pretty good luck."

When we got closer to the cabin at the end of the day, we set some small snares for snowshoe hares. Here, Grandpa Liam showed me one set and had me do the rest. "We can check the main lines every other day, but the snowshoe sets need to be checked every day otherwise the lynx, bobcats, fishers, and owls will eat your kills."

Back at the cabin, we ate the last of the pork chops with a can of cream corn. It wasn't Grandma Emma's cooking, but I was so hungry it made Grandpa Liam seem like a top gourmet chef. Even Sean Sherman, who won awards as a famous Native cook and went by the name "The Sioux Chef," couldn't have matched this.

After we finished dinner Grandpa Liam set a kerosene lantern at the kitchen table and told me to sit and look at my homework assignments. I was so tired, the idea of opening a book or reading someone else's words sounded terrible.

I took the notebooks that Nora had given me out of my backpack and decided to write for just a minute or two. In the first notebook, I started jotting down notes about the Schroeder case. I wrote about Grandma

Emma's burn and my plan to get Grandpa Liam to talk about that. I wrote about my dad's conversation with my Grandpa Liam in the screened-in porch back at Red Gut and how suspicious they sounded. Who were Ethan and Olivia? Why were they keeping secrets?

Then I opened the second notebook and decided that I would use it like Dumbledore's Pensieve in the Harry Potter books. I started to write down my own memories. I wrote about Matt Schroeder and when he attacked me at the summer camp. I wrote about Nora, how beautiful she looked in her Toronto Maple Leafs beanie, how smart she was in class with Mr. Lukas, how radiant she was in her jingle dress at the summer pow-wows, and how I wanted her to be so much more than my best friend.

I decided to follow her advice too and tried to write about my mom. I started with how my mind went blank when I tried to think of her and all I could conjure was picture-like memories. Then, all of a sudden, the memories started to come back, fast and then faster. I started writing as quickly as I could, so I wouldn't forget them. My mom was a fireball—quick to laugh and quick to anger, petite and wiry. She was born in the Indian Health Service Clinic at White Earth but had been raised in foster care. She'd lived with three foster families and a group home by the time she turned eighteen. Once she was old enough to work, that was all she really knew. She worked at the Roy Lake Store throughout high school. By the time she graduated, my mom had a deep sense of independence. She moved to Minneapolis when she finished high school, working at the American Indian Center on Franklin, Powwow Grounds Coffee, and then Erickson Lumber.

My dad must have seemed like everything my mom missed out on when she grew up. He came from a stable, loving family. He was calm and reliable and he liked to stay home. They'd both wanted a big family. But after I was born, my mom had health complications, and though I never knew all the details, I did know that she had a number of miscarriages. My baby brothers and sisters just never made it into this world. It was really hard on her and they eventually decided that I was all they really needed. I guess I loved them both for that, even though I didn't know enough to say so in those years.

When I was little, my mom always seemed to have everything under control. She ran our house like an air traffic controller on Thanksgiving Day—calendars, schedules, text reminders, chore lists. It was probably as annoying for my dad as it was for me because we both got a chore list from her every Sunday morning. But he adored my mom, even when she was being bossy, and he was always jumping into action to do something to please her. I remembered the adoring look on her face when she danced with him in the living room.

My mom was the one who showed me how to pop wild rice and make cabbage soup. I recalled the time we went to help at Porky White's sugarbush in Maple Plain. She made me haul a full five-gallon pail of sap in each hand, admonishing me not to spill a drop, then throwing snowballs at me, knowing I couldn't set them down. We all had a big laugh when I was finally able to set the pails down safely. I always knew she loved me. I marched to the sound of her soprano voice. We all did. She came to all my school conferences and watched every fight with me.

I glanced up from writing long enough to notice that Grandpa Liam had shut off his kerosene lamp and gone to bed. My fingers were starting to ache from writing so fast, but I couldn't stop. Everything was coming back, even the night I first learned my mom was sick. I'd opened my bedroom door, snuck down the stairs, and sat on the staircase just above the kitchen so I could eavesdrop from the shadows. My dad was sitting in one of the dining chairs wearing khaki pants, Doc Martens, and a blue MCTC polo. His hands dwarfed the tea cup he clutched. My mom was pacing around the kitchen in a pair of Hokas and sport pants, her oversized yellow tee shirt billowing with movement.

"Byron, I'm seriously sick. The chances aren't that good, with or without it. This kind of leukemia is really aggressive."

From the shadows of my perch on the stairs I could see the pained look on his face. "Isabelle, you need to fight this. You need to understand that you are the backbone of this family. It doesn't work without you. You've been showing up for us every day, for all of Ezra's years on earth. We need you."

I crept back upstairs, my white crew socks silent on the oak-floored hallway to my room. I lay in bed wondering what I just heard. The thought that we might lose my mom was terrifying. I tossed and turned all night long.

My parents had sat me down in the living room the next morning and tried to explain. Mom was on the verge of tears, so my dad did most of the talking. I watched his weighty frame as it sunk into the sofa. He pressed his hands together to stop them from trembling.

"Ezra, your mom is sick. It's cancer and it's in her blood and spreading to other parts of her body. The doctors are getting her started on chemo. But . . . there's a good chance she's not going to make it."

I stared at him. I had no idea what to say. It felt like there was acid in my throat, like after puking. I didn't know if they were waiting for me to cry or scream or what. I mainly just felt confused, and a little sick to my stomach.

My dad gave a little groan as he pulled himself out of the sofa. Both he and my mom came to give me a hug. "We will be okay, Ezra. We'll find a way," he whispered. I'm not sure if he was trying to convince me, my mom, or himself.

I lost track of time writing in spite of my exhaustion. As I regained self awareness, I realized that I was clammy with sweat. I felt washed out, like I had just finished crying. I closed the notebook and looked around. Grandpa Liam was in his bedroll with Buster curled up next to him, fast asleep and snoring. I whispered, "Buster, you're a fickle traitor. You were supposed to sleep with me!" But I didn't mean it. Buster and Grandpa Liam had belonged to each other since that dog was born. I was the newcomer, and both had done nothing but welcome me.

I sat on the edge of the bed for a minute and reopened my notebook. I had several pages of notes. Grandpa was still snoring so I read them all out loud. Then I pushed a strand of the white, wispy hair from my grandfather's forehead, shut off the kerosene lamp, and went to bed.

Chapter 15

GRANDPA LIAM was the fastest seventy-four-year-old man I had ever witnessed in the woods. It was our third day out on the trapline. Now that all the traps were set, we sped the snow machine down the south loop road. We still had the game sled, axes, hatchets, and the chainsaw. We had large burlap bags now too, and rope. We brought the waterproof insulated gloves and two rifles. The .22 Winchester Magnum Rimfire was a small caliber rifle and Grandpa Liam brought that in case there was a wounded animal in one of the traps. The 7mm Remington Magnum was in case we ran into a moose or whitetail deer. Grandpa Liam said that I could shoot if we got an opportunity. The rifles were cased and in the sled, but I was still intently scanning the woods for any sign of big game.

The stick was down at our second set. Grandpa Liam stopped the Ski-Doo but left it idle.

"Grab the burlap bag, Ez. Come behind me and step in my tracks."

I followed behind him through the hazel brush, tag alder, and poplar saplings. The snare wire was taut, but I couldn't see any animal until Grandpa Liam gave the wire a firm tug, pulling the frozen form of a large lynx from the snow.

"You got one, Grandpa."

He turned and smiled. I saw him pull off his mittens and take a pouch of tobacco out of his pocket. "Miigwech zhawenimiyan. Gibiindaakoonin weweni."

He put the tobacco on the ground and slid the snare from the lynx's neck. "Put her in the bag, Ez. Then retrace your steps and tie the bag in the sled. I'll reset this and be right there."

Grandpa Liam was smooth in the brush, which slid off his coat without issue as he returned to the Ski-Doo. Then, "Let's go, grandson!"

Grandpa Liam punched the accelerator. He was running the Ski-Doo like he was shooting for time trials at Cain's Quest Snowmobile Race. His reserved and cautious road driving was done: he was running the line, and it was a long one for short winter days. Our trail from setting the traps was packing in nicely and the machine gripped the trail without issue. We could see our footsteps where we'd set trails and looked out for Grandpa Liam's stakes.

I was surprised at how successful our efforts were. Every third set seemed to have something. He had me release the number two traps for marten and mink and reset those. And he showed me how to reset the fox snares. He had me carry our kills in the burlap bags, rather than drag animals in the snow. We carefully stepped in our previous footprints back and forth. The less disturbance the better. The beaver sets were a little more work. We had to re-chop the ice because of freeze-over and then use a stick on each one to see if there was a beaver in the Conibear. When there was, we had to pull the entire set out to release it and then reset the trap, the stakes, and the hole. Then we kicked snow over the opening to block light. Grandpa said we could get many beavers out of one lodge on the same set.

When we finished on the south loop, we drove the north loop. Those sets were made the previous day, so we didn't get as many there. But we made both loops in a little over half a day. Buster was happy to have us back early at the cabin.

The day's work was really still ahead. We drank tea and brought animals in one at a time to work on them on the kitchen table. Grandpa preferred them to be slightly frozen, so the job wasn't too messy.

Each animal had certain parts—organs or joints—that had to go back in the woods or the water with tobacco offerings. The skinning and stretching of hides were slower and more meticulous. Grandpa Liam showed me what to do, but I was so worried about cutting holes in the hides that he got two or three done in the time it took me to do one.

"That's the way. I'd rather have them done right than right now. You'll get faster as you get more experience."

Once we settled into a cadence with skinning, scraping and stretching hides, and processing beaver meat, Grandpa Liam started telling stories again.

"Ezra, there is only one animal in all these woods that would challenge the wolf pack."

"What animal is that?"

"Usually bears avoid wolves. An alpha wolf like Ogimaa probably weighs eighty kilograms. That's one hundred and seventy-five pounds for you Americans." He chuckled and slapped me on the shoulder. "That is a huge animal. Bigger than me. Adult black bears weigh anywhere from sixty to three hundred kilograms. That's about one hundred and thirty to six hundred and sixty pounds for Americans." He chuckled again. The same jokes worked over and over with him. "Most bears are smaller or the same size as a wolf. Some of the older ones are bigger, but not bigger than any three wolves together. And a wolf pack is usually a dozen animals. Sometimes a really healthy pack like the one at Chief's Ridge could be closer to twenty. One-on-one, a bear might have an advantage, but wolves come in packs. Bears know this. They don't mess with wolves. They are totally out-matched. But once in a while there is an anomaly—an exception to the general rules of the forest. The world record black bear weighed five hundred kilograms—one thousand and one hundred pounds—and was two and half meters long. That animal was killed in 1972. The size sounds prehistoric, but it was real."

His brow wrinkled as he continued, "There is one bear in these parts that's even bigger than that. We don't even call him Makwa, for Bear. We call him Chi-awesiinh. That means Big Animal. That's his name. And he earned it. Chi for short. He is so huge, and so mean, that the wolves won't even mess with him. And wolves, especially a strong pack like this one, usually feel like it's their right to mess with anything they want. Two trappers were killed in bear attacks east of here over the past several years. There's a hollow there and caves in the side of the hill. I think that's where Chi usually sleeps in the winter. We can't say for sure it was him, but I don't doubt it. One party tried to track him, but as huge as he is, he is just as wily as he is mean. We thought about bringing tribal hunters from Red Gut and Seine River to look for him, but the risk was too high. We decided to leave him be. But that is one animal we never want to tangle with."

"Grandpa, what if he comes here? He could push the door right off the hinges."

Grandpa Liam laughed. "He sure could. But bears sleep in the winter. Sometimes we call it hibernation, but bears don't actually hibernate. Hibernation means lowering the body temperature and heart rate. They just sleep for six months—half the year. Lucky for us, they sleep from October through March. We pull traps in March before Chi wakes up. I've never had a problem. It's January now, so that's about as safe as it gets."

Once we finished with the hides, we hung the beaver stretchers on the wall and leaned the fox stretchers in the corner. They would dry out best with the heat of the stove. We cut and processed beaver meat, sealing pieces in Ziploc bags. These we stashed in a large box in the shed so they'd freeze, and hoisted two large logs on top to prevent animals from getting at the meat.

"If we keep going like this," he said, "I might have to open my earthen food cache early."

Chapter 16

WE GOT INTO A flow after that third day. We checked the line every other day, and the rabbit snares daily. Snowshoe hares were prey for many animals and Grandpa Liam wanted our sets checked often so they wouldn't steal our kills. In the afternoons and off days, we worked on hides. I did homework then too. We only had disruptions when it snowed more than a couple of inches, which forced us to reset the snares. And we started to eat beaver meat with our meals after that. It was pretty good with oatmeal in the morning. Any bones or parts that we couldn't use got loaded into the sled and we brought them out in the woods and left them there with tobacco offerings. The sacred parts of the animals were put as offerings either in the woods, for most of the animals, or in the water for the beavers and muskrats.

Grandpa was right about raiders taking the kills from my rabbit snares. There were tracks everywhere. He usually made me check those solo and I wasn't really skilled at identifying the animals. Maybe coyotes or wolves did it, I thought. Finally, I brought Grandpa Liam with me to check.

"No sensible coyote would come into these parts. The wolves would kill them. I think you have wolves hitting the rabbit snares. It's unusual, but not unheard of."

"What should we do?"

"Well, Ezra. We are wolf clan. So the wolf is the only animal in the woods we are forbidden to kill. You'll have to let them have their way. They'll probably get bored or hungry and go after bigger game anyways."

"I read a book by Farley Mowat called *Never Cry Wolf*. The guy in that book drank pots of tea and peed everywhere to mark his territory and the wolves peed where he peed and accepted his claim."

Grandpa Liam laughed. "Ezra, you're a charming boy. But Farley Mowat's book is fiction. It's make-believe. I will admit, for a white guy, he seemed to have his head screwed on straight about the sacredness of wolves. But there's no way the wolves will play along with you and leave your snares alone based on where you pee."

"You read *Never Cry Wolf*?" I guess I shouldn't have been surprised.

"I read all the books on the shelves of our cabin. I've been reading daily, since I was a little kid. My dad did too. He's the one who made it a habit for me. A lot of trappers read like this. We entertain each other with stories when we're together, and we entertain ourselves by reading when we're alone."

"You know so much about the woods, Grandpa. I never really knew until now that you were so book smart too."

He squeezed my shoulder for a second. "Tomorrow we'll go hunting. You can come out here and pee by your snares wherever you want before we go."

I guess stubbornness runs in our family. I got up at first light and started drinking tea. I waited until my bladder felt ready to burst, then I took two mason jars to the outhouse and nearly filled them both. I figured I'd save myself a lot of trouble and mark my rabbit territory in a few minutes. I walked them over to the snares and went in a wide circle around the area, dropping a little pee every ten feet or so. After that, I walked the perimeter again just a few feet out from where I'd peed and put a small piece of beaver meat every ten feet or so. I wasn't sure if any of this would have any effect, but if there was even the smallest chance that I could prove Grandpa Liam wrong, I was determined to do it.

Grandpa Liam was waiting outside, gassing up the Ski-Doo when I got back to the cabin. "Change into your camouflage clothes. It's hunting time."

I felt a surge of adrenaline as I moved with determined precision through the mundane tasks of brushing my teeth and donning my hunting clothes. It took me just a minute or two to load the gear and jump on the Ski-Doo. We had the sled, but no tools or supplies except for two knives, one hatchet, and the 7mm. Grandpa Liam had me drive down the south loop road for a couple miles and then cut across one of the ponds there through the deep snow. He tacked up a bright orange target against a spruce tree and then we motored about one hundred yards out on the lake. I had practiced shooting with Grandpa Liam once in a while in the summer, but he gave me refresher on the bolt action and clip for the 7mm as well as the safety and scope. He had me lean over the Ski-Doo, carefully bracing my arms, and breath slowly, pulling the trigger once in the middle of my breath. We did that four times. The recoil from the 7mm wasn't so bad with all my layers of clothing, but the sharp report of the rifle rung in my ears. He had a pair of binoculars in his coat and watched my bullet placement, then we checked the target. Everything landed on the target, but one bullet pulled low and left.

"I think you were anticipating the kick on your first shot. If we can get you up on a moose or deer, just keep your cool and shoot like you did right here."

We took the Ski-Doo to the other end of the pond and there was a massive beaver dam there. Grandpa Liam took a blaze-orange ribbon from his coat pocket and tied it as high as he could reach on a willow sapling.

"If anything exciting happens today, it's easy to get turned around out here. Some of the ponds look a lot alike. This can help you spot your places even in poor light."

We left the Ski-Doo and started walking along the creek. It was too brushy for snowshoes, but the snow was past my knees and slow walking. The creek below the beaver dam was frozen over, but it widened as we went. After forty-five minutes of walking, I was sweating like a tiny tot at the Leech Lake Fourth of July Powwow. We stopped at a grove of cedar trees. "Let's crawl in here," Grandpa said. In the thicket of cedar, we were completely disguised. Grandpa broke a couple of branches so we could have a view of the creek.

"Look down there," he said. "There are springs in the creek here and the ice is weak. It's open much of the year. The otters use the opening to come on the ice from time to time. Moose like it here because they are so big; it's a lot of work to eat enough snow to stay hydrated. They like the open water spot for drinking. And in the winter, they eat cedar buds and hazel brush instead of grass and lily pad roots."

Grandpa Liam handed me the rifle, directed me to chamber a round, and put the safety on. Then he lay down on the cedar branches he'd broken off for my view window and fell fast asleep.

It must have been a good sleep too, because I think he snored loud enough to scare away all the animals in the forest. There was an otter that kept popping up through the little opening in the ice, but I didn't see anything else.

So, I started thinking about Nora. I wondered if she was scared back in Northeast. Was everything okay down there? I wondered about my dad too. I probably stressed him out. I knew I hadn't been very warm with him. My head dropped for a minute—just long enough to realize that my toes were cold.

A loud crash jerked me out of my head. I strained my eyes, scanning the shoreline. What was that? There, not thirty yards away, a young bull moose emerged from the thicket and started walking across the ice toward the otter hole. Even with his thick, dark winter coat, his musculature seemed to ripple in the winter sun. His horns were smaller than an older bull, but his body was enormous. I wanted to kick Grandpa Liam so he could coach me through this. But there wasn't time.

I shouldered the rifle and put the crosshairs on the moose. His fur was blacker than charcoal and the crosshairs of the rifle were too. I couldn't even see where to aim. I just kept the rifle up and slowly followed his path. The angle improved, and finally I could see the crosshairs. I breathed in, held, and slowly exhaled. The rifle cracked in the crisp winter air. I saw the hind legs of the moose kick once, like a horse trying to buck off a rider at the Calgary Stampede, and then he ran.

I turned to see if Grandpa Liam was awake. He must have been up for a while because he was standing behind me. He slapped me on the shoulder. "You got him, Ezra. You got him."

"But he ran away."

"A bull moose can weigh as much as five hundred and forty kilograms. That's twelve hundred pounds to you. They can run with a bullet straight through the heart for a long distance. But they only kick like that when they're hit in the heart or aorta. Let's go have a look."

We went out to where the moose had been standing when I shot him. And sure enough, there was a tuft of hair and small spatter of blood in the snow. Grandpa Liam dropped an orange ribbon there and packed some snow around one end, so it wouldn't blow away. We followed the path the moose took and pretty soon we found a clear blood trail. It got bigger as we went, a crescendo of vermilion jets unmistakable in the pure, white snow. And there, just inside the tree line on the far shore, the moose was lying, his enormous body prostrate and motionless.

Grandpa Liam clapped me on the back and handed me a pouch of tobacco. "You'll make two offerings here. The second one will be later, to the creator and the spirits, and you'll make that with his sacred parts after you've cut the meat and organs. But the first you make to the moose that you harvested. Hold the tobacco in your left hand. That one's closest to your heart. And you speak to this moose and give him thanks. Tell him you're sorry. And promise him that you won't waste his hide or body. Tell him you did this so you could provide for the people."

"Do I have to do this in Ojibwe?"

"You have to do this from your heart."

I hesitated and then tried my best to say everything I could in our language. "Miigwech aapiji zhawenimi-yan. Onjida inga-aabajitoon giwiiyaas ji-bami'agwaa nii-janishinaabeg. Gaawiin inga-nishwanaajitoosiin giiyaw." I pulled it off, but it made me want to pay more attention to Grandpa Liam, Grandma Emma, and my dad when they were speaking our language. Grandpa Liam seemed pleased.

"Now the real work begins. Ezra, we only have a few hours of light, and you shot one of the biggest moose in the entire treaty area. Skinning and quartering without a block and tackle is going to take some time."

He motioned and talked me through the process, working side-by-side. We gutted him first. I had been around animal harvesting for years, but usually it was piles of hides on stretchers or boxes in Grandpa Liam's screened-in porch. I had never shot an animal before. And I had never seen so much blood in one place. The body was warm and gave a distinct smell. It wasn't a bad smell, but it was visceral and penetrating, like hot cedar tea, mud, and body odor mixed together, overwhelming my other senses. For some reason, it reminded me of the dream I had back in Northeast where I was hunting with the wolves.

"Grandpa, would the wolves take our kill?"

"Any wolf would be delighted to eat your kill. But they really don't attack humans. If we are here, they'll keep their distance. But you can be sure that when night falls there will be animals all over this place—fox, fisher, and wolf. First come, first served to anything we leave behind."

After gutting, we skinned him, rolling the large body side to side until we worked it off. Then we used the knives to cut the meat into quarters, strip the backstraps and loins, cut the briskets, and trim smaller cuts from the ribcage. We had to use a hatchet to cut the hind quarter ball joints, but everything else was easily done with a simple knife. It still took us an hour.

"Ezra, I'm sending you back after the Ski-Doo. Just follow our tracks and you'll find it easily enough. Then come and get me. You won't be able to come the same way. There are way too many deadfalls and too much brush. And you won't be able to come up the creek from the Twin Lake landing down the trail. There are too many springs in the creek and you'll put the Ski-Doo and yourself straight through the ice and that'll be the end of you both. You'll have to double back on the south loop trail to the cabin. From there, it's a short cut through the woods to Pickerel Lake. You just go right down the chain of lakes where we've been setting beaver traps on until you find me here. There's either a creek or portage between each one, so go slow there. The ice should be fine."

"What are you going to do?"

"I'm going to finish my nap."

"What?"

He chuckled. "I am going to skid your kill out onto the ice and keep the animals away until you get here. Be careful but don't waste time. When you get to the cabin, grab Buster and bring him with. We'll be away from the snares and if you have any trouble at all, he'll be more help than the entire Royal Canadian Mounted Police."

I was a sweaty mess by the time I made it back to the Ski-Doo. I had driven it with Grandpa Liam but never by myself. And I had never taken the route he'd described by myself either. What if I got lost? What if I crashed the machine? What if the animals got my kill before I could get over there?

I could see the orange ribbon Grandpa Liam had tied above the trailhead from three hundred yards away. I fired up the Ski-Doo and made it back to the main trail. Then I opened it up. If I hadn't been so stressed out about navigating back to the kill site I would have enjoyed that ride even more. My eyes started to water as I rocketed across the hard-packed south loop trail to the clearing by the cabin. I let go of the throttle and brought the machine to a stop so I could wipe the water out.

On my periphery, I caught a faint movement at the far edge of the clearing where my rabbit snare line was— just a little flash of brown and gray. I turned my gaze to the movement and froze, stiffer than a walleye pike left overnight in a tip-up hole. There were four wolves standing at the far edge of the clearing. Two were mottled gray with black streaks, one darker brown, and one a light gray, so light it almost looked white.

"Ogimaa," I whispered.

Chapter 17

THE HAIR ON THE back of my neck stood straight up. Grandpa had said that wolves didn't mess with humans. But even if I opened up the throttle on the Ski-Doo full blast, they could probably reach the cabin before I did. I didn't move a muscle, but neither did they. They were staring right at me.

There was nothing I could do but follow Grandpa Liam's directions. I slowly accelerated the Ski-Doo, right up to the door of the cabin. I left it running and hopped off. I kept facing the wolves and walked backward to the door, opening it just enough for Buster to come out. Then I got back on the Ski-Doo, swooped up Buster, tucked him in my coat with just his head sticking out, and sped off toward Pickerel Lake. I had to slow down by the lakeshore to make sure I didn't catch on any unseen logs below the snow cover. But once I was on Pickerel, I opened the throttle up wide. I glanced over my shoulder a few times, but it looked like the wolves hadn't moved once from the time I first saw them.

It took a while for my heartbeat to come back down. Then I started to think. Grandpa Liam must have been crazy to trust a fifteen-year-old kid with his Ski-Doo, solo, on a wilderness route he had never traveled before. A lot of things could go wrong. I really hoped that I wouldn't mess this up. It would be a disaster if I got lost or we lost all the meat from my first kill. I was thinking about the wolves too. What if they decided to come after Buster? What if they were checking my rabbit snares again? Maybe my *Never Cry Wolf* plan would work?

In spite of all my stressing, Grandpa Liam's instructions were pretty solid. I recognized the beaver house on the south shore of Pickerel and found a little portage into the next pond there. The lakes and ponds got smaller as I navigated the chain. We had set beaver traps on many of them. I only slowed down for the portages and beaver dams. The sun was setting and the dense cloud cover was darkening quickly when I saw the silhouette of Grandpa Liam at the edge of the next pond. True to his word, he had dragged the moose quarters, backstraps, head, and hide to the lake. I motored up and then shut off the Ski-Doo, dismounted, and gave him a tight hug, accidentally squishing Buster between us.

He laughed and looked at me quizzically. "Everything okay, Ezra?"

"Yeah. I have a story for you, but it can wait."

"Okay."

We lifted the pieces into the sled with Buster dancing in circles in excitement.

"All right, Ezra, take this tobacco and grab those," Grandpa Liam said. He pointed to a dark red piece of meat and a ball of fur on the ice.

"What is that?"

"Every animal has a special part, a sacred part, that we don't eat. On some animals, it's the liver. On others, it's a different organ. This is the one for the moose. You have to put that in a bush or tree as high as he walks with your tobacco. And you put these too." He reached down and grabbed the piece of fur, placing it in my hand. It must have weighed half a pound.

"What is this?"

"His nuts."

"What?"

"Those are his male parts." Grandpa Liam was straight-faced and unflinching.

"Oh my God! Grandpa!"

Then he burst into laughter. "Yes, grandson. Those are his testicles. The whole package really, frank and beans."

"You can't be serious. Is this some joke you play on all people who get their first kill?"

"If it were a joke, I'd make you eat them for supper. This is for real. His male parts are sacred too. Really. You are going put those in a tree too with tobacco. The first prayer you made right after you shot was to the moose. This time, you pray to our Creator and all the spirits around us to bless the moose nation to be numerous and healthy. You look out for the moose now the way this one looked out for you."

I did what I was told. I found a thick tag alder and put his sacred parts there. I put tobacco down and I prayed. I prayed for the moose nation, for the forest, for our treaty lands, for this sacred place. I prayed it would all be safe from the mines and logging and pollution—from all the dirty snow and everything that caused it everywhere else.

When I made it back to the Ski-Doo, I cranked the ratchet straps to make sure none of our meat would fall out on the ride back to the cabin. It wasn't until after I looked up that I noticed the strange look on Grandpa Liam's face.

"What?"

"You're a fine young man, Ezra. You're my family. You're a successful hunter now. But it's more than that. You're a success as a man."

I didn't know what to say to that.

"You can drive us back, Ezra."

The last light was fading from the sky, so I turned on the Ski-Doo lights and drove us carefully back through the chain of lakes toward home. As I navigated up the bank from Pickerel, I thought I saw shadows in the dark, racing across the lake, back toward the kill site.

IT WAS COMPLETELY DARK when we got to the cabin and all the excitement and effort had left me hungrier than I'd ever been. We didn't have time to cut ice for Grandpa's storage cache, so we put the moose quarters on the roof of the cabin for the morning.

"It'll be safe there until morning. The eagles and vultures don't fly at night, and the only animal crazy enough to come after it is Chi, and he's sleeping in his den kilometers from here." Grandpa seemed sure, but I knew I'd feel a lot better when we had everything stowed away in the cache tomorrow.

It took Grandpa about ten minutes to stoke the fire and heat up the corned beef hash and baked beans on the Drolet. I practically inhaled my supper. Nothing had tasted so good. When I finally caught my breath and the food hit my belly, I told Grandpa Liam about the wolves.

"I still think there's no way they peed everywhere you did to accept your territory around those snares. But we'll give it a good look in the morning before we check traps."

I boiled water in the tea kettle and poured a cup for each of us, adding tea bags, and tried to work up a little more courage.

"Grandpa, can I ask you a question?"

"Anything."

"When we were back at the rez, right before we came to Chief's Ridge, you told me you were in Northeast Minneapolis before."

"Well, we were. We were there several times. We came down for your birth, for a couple of your early birthdays, and we were there after you punched that locker. We never liked the city. We never trusted the people there. But we always loved you."

"Wait . . . so you were in the city the night of the fire?" I had thought it was him, but I needed to know for sure. I tilted my head, trying to read his body language as well as his words.

Grandpa Liam stiffened for just a second, but he seemed nonplussed as he responded. He looked right at me with eyes kind and unflinching. "Yes. We came to convince Byron to come back here with you. The city swallowed up two of your cousins and your mom, each in different ways. We didn't want it to take you too. Those Schroeder people were awful and we were worried about you. If they didn't get you, the drugs would, or the gangs, or the justice system."

I was hurt now. I could feel my body tense in response. "Grandpa, I'm stronger than that."

"I'm sorry Ez. I can see that now."

My anger made me bolder. "Did you start the fire?"

"No way. If I wanted to take somebody out, I'd do something way more dramatic."

He laughed and—upset though I was—I couldn't help but smile. I let out a big breath.

"But I . . . What about that burn scar on Grandma's hand?"

Grandpa Liam studied my face for a second before he answered that one. I thought I might have overstepped asking that question so directly. "She burned that pulling the bannock pan from the oven weeks before the Schroeder fire."

I couldn't think of any reason not to believe him. "Grandpa, I've been trying to figure out who killed the Schroeders. Everyone seemed to think it could be me. At least it felt like that. Detective Williams. Matt Schroeder. Even my dad."

"Why do you think we're out here, Ezra?"

I ignored the question.

"I feel like nobody trusts me."

"Your dad wants you to have a long, healthy, happy life. With you in Canada, someone like Detective Williams can't make a rush judgment. He'll have to complete his investigation before they make any arrests. They'll find the culprit, if it wasn't actually an accident, and you'll be safe and out of trouble until they do."

"So sending me here was my dad's version of sending me to the juvenile detention center?"

"Don't be a fool, grandson. Your dad sent you here because he wants you to know our ways, and because I've been begging him to do it for your entire life. Your dad stayed up all night the night of the fire, pacing the hallway outside your door and keeping vigil in the kitchen. He was worried about your injury and the effect of the pain meds they gave you. He knew your heart and your whereabouts the entire night."

"If he knew where I was, why did he even have to ask me?"

"I think he wanted to see if you'd lie, you know . . . to cover for a friend."

"Nora?"

"Your dad is clever like that."

"Not clever enough. She would never hurt somebody, even to protect herself."

"Are you sure about that?"

"Positive."

Now I was mad at my dad *and* my grandpa. He grabbed a book off the shelf on the north wall and shuffled to his bed with Buster and a kerosene lamp. I took out my notebooks and sat at the table after that. In one I added the information about Grandma Emma's burn and the whereabouts of all the Clouds on the night of the fire. But I didn't write down any suspicions of Nora. That was ridiculous. In the other notebook, I wrote about my big day. Somehow putting everything down in that notebook softened my anger toward Grandpa Liam. He was just being honest and answering my questions, even if he was wrong. I threw a couple logs into the Drolet and went to bed. Buster and Grandpa Liam were already lost in slumber.

Chapter 18

WE WERE UP AT first light. There was so much to do. Breakfast was wild rice with dried cranberries. We used powdered milk to mix with water and added a little maple syrup.

I had to finish sorting out the moose meat before we did anything else. We dressed light in preparation for hard physical labor rather than the normal layers of trapping clothes. I wore Dickies and muck boots with a lighter jacket. Grandpa Liam wore his canvas Carhartt bibs and Under Armour, but no jacket. We took the chainsaw and two sets of log skidding tongs down to Manidookaan and cut big blocks of ice from the lake, pulling and skidding them until we could get them in the game sled. Then we hurried back to the cabin to set them in the food cache, moved all the moose meat there, and packed it with more ice blocks and then sawdust. It really was a clever way to keep the stash frozen and impossible for animals to get at. We also had to spend some time working on the moose head. The moose's beard we kept for medicine. We used the chainsaw to separate the antlers from the skull. Then we saved the brain, which was just warm enough still not to be frozen solid.

"We'll use that to soften the hide when we tan it," Grandpa Liam said.

After that, we checked my rabbit snares. I had four snowshoe hares in the snares and not a single set was raided. On the outside of my perimeter there were wolf tracks everywhere. My plan had worked. I could feel the warm glow of satisfaction deep in my gut as I waited for Grandpa Liam to notice.

"Look, Ezra. They didn't mark your spots, but they didn't raid your snares either. It's amazing!"

"I actually put little pieces of beaver meat on the other side of my perimeter," I smiled.

Grandpa Liam studied the tracks intently for several minutes, moving in a slow circle along my perimeter and then looking at me with newfound respect. "Ahhh. It's still amazing. It's like they accepted that meat as an offering and agreed to stay on their side of your line. It's really hard to believe. This is even harder for me to say, but . . . you were right and I was wrong."

"I wasn't totally right."

"But you weren't totally wrong, either."

I smiled again.

"I'd still recommend not setting out more food for them. They might start to expect it. Let's see how you do snaring with just one offering for the wolves."

"Okay."

We grabbed snow bibs and trapping coats and headed off to check the rest of the traps and snares. The cloud cover disappeared and the bright, pale winter sun reflected off the snow. It was so bright that it was painful to look around. The snow glittered and dazzled. It even looked like there was a circular rainbow around the sun.

"Grandpa, what does that mean?" It seemed like it might be of spiritual importance.

"That's a sun dog. It means it's going to be cold."

I looked for a smile or sign that he was just messing with me, but he just kept rummaging in his backpack without a second glance. Then he handed me a pair of sunglasses.

"Put these on, Ezra."

They definitely weren't cool. I looked like I'd stole Dwight Schrute's nerd glasses from the set of *The Office* and had them shaded just for this. Grandpa Liam's looked more like Wes Studi's profile picture on the cover of *GQ*. At least Nora wasn't here to see this.

We spent the rest of the day on the loops. The north loop seemed to produce more success than the south this time. By the time we got back my body was complaining. Between hauling the moose into the cache, skidding ice blocks, and pulling and resetting beaver traps, my back was shot.

"That'll give you a true Ojibwe build, Ezra. Your neck, back, and shoulders will grow strong. I bet Nora will like that."

"That joke was old the second time you said it! And that was a dozen jokes ago! She's just a friend, Grandpa!"

"Okay . . ." he drew out. But he still laughed.

The clear sky and sun dog meant cold weather coming. There wasn't a cloud around to hold the heat when the sun set. Grandpa Liam loaded the Drolet up after supper and started putting on layers of clothes.

"Ezra, lets walk down to Manidookaan. We're going to get a show tonight."

Tired though I was, I donned my heavy clothes again without complaint. We walked all the way down to Manidookaan rather than use the Ski-Doo. We left Buster behind.

Grandpa Liam was right. The northern lights were arcing and dancing in the night sky. We walked out onto the lake, far enough so the shoreline looked like a dark, jagged line far in the distance. Then Grandpa Liam motioned and dropped to his knees.

I got down to see if something was wrong, but he just pulled a tiny birchbark basket out of his pocket. It was just big enough to hold a spoonful of wild rice with a little maple syrup on top. He put it right on the ice, and packed a little snow around it so it wouldn't blow or tip over. Then he put some tobacco there.

"Gimikwenimaanaanig gidinawemaaganinaanig gaa-aandakiijig. For our relatives on the other side. We remember you and offer you this food." His face looked solemn, and, in the glow of the northern lights, perhaps a little older.

We lay down on the ice on our backs, still warm and insulated in our heavy coats, bibs, and layers. The northern lights continued to oscillate green and blue with an occasional flash of yellow or orange. I had never seen anything quite so beautiful.

"Grandpa, do you miss your parents and the other people who changed worlds—the ones on the other side, dancing up there?"

"My sweet boy. I miss them more than words can tell. The older I get, the more people I know on the other side. I'm not lonely because I have Emma and you and your dad. But I feel loss and longing. I'm patient, you know. I'm happy to wait until my time comes. Life is sweet. Watching you become a man fills me with joy, Ezra. I don't want to miss anything. I hope you'll be patient with your time too. You have so much to live for, and so many people who love you."

"I've been so mad at my dad."

"I can see that."

"I feel like he should have stopped my mom from working at the pulp factory. He should have known."

"You might not believe me, Ezra, but your mom loved her job at Erickson. She actually made more money than your dad. It must have given her a sense of independence and empowerment. That means a lot to people, especially when they had a childhood like hers. It's probably the main reason your folks stayed in Northeast. You know your dad would have been happy to teach Ojibwe at Rainy River Community College in International Falls or Seven Generations Education Institute in Fort Frances, so he could be a little closer to Red Gut."

I must have looked incredulous.

"Ezra, your parents had no way of knowing that the pulp mill could make your mom sick."

I sighed.

Grandpa Liam studied my face for a minute and added, "I think your dad did the best he could. You know, Ezra, he loves you most of all."

We stayed like that for a long time, listening to the wind whistle through the pines on the distant shore, watching the kaleidoscope of color dancing in the sky, and maybe both of us thinking about my mom and Grandpa Liam's parents, Nora's dad, and all our family in this world and the next. Just for a moment, I felt a little twinge of pain in the scar on my left hand run down my arm and toward my heart.

Chapter 19

GRANDPA LIAM and I got into a steady rhythm the next three weeks. We woke with the sun, ate, and started working. We checked traps every other day and those were full days. We cut, hauled, split, stacked firewood, and worked on hides on the off days.

I checked my rabbit snares every day. The wolves continued to leave them alone, which gave me a tremendous sense of satisfaction. It wasn't just that I had surprised Grandpa Liam. It felt like the wolves and I had an understanding.

We had three big snowstorms that month too, each dumping at least half a foot of snow. Whenever it stormed we had to reset all the snares. The marten and fisher sets were fine in the trees and the beaver sets were fine in the water, but everything else needed adjustments. My little rabbit snares were buried. Grandpa Liam let me work all the resets though. When they kept producing, he let me do more. It felt like something had shifted. I knew what I was doing. Grandpa Liam seemed to think I knew what I was doing too.

Every evening I had to read and do homework. I wrote more in my notebooks too. It gave me some relief to hear that Grandpa Liam and Grandma Emma actually were in Northeast Minneapolis, but that they had nothing to do with the fire. I believed Grandpa Liam about that and the cause of the burn on Grandma Emma's palm. I figured it would be helpful to verify that some other way, too, in case anyone else suspected them. I still couldn't get that image out of my head of Matt Schroeder pointing at me and yelling. I added a little every day, hoping that I might see something in a different way and get a breakthrough.

I couldn't wait to hear what Nora had learned. I hoped she was safe. I wrote in the other notebook even more. In addition to my secrets about summer camp and the flood of memories about my mom, I started writing everything I loved about Nora—the shape of her slender fingers, her laugh, the way she flicked her hair out of the way when she was working in a textbook.

"February is the coldest and least snowy month of the winter, Ezra." Every time I put down a book or pencil in the evening, Grandpa Liam tried to impart some kind of wisdom while we were both still awake.

"It sure feels like it."

"We are going to have company tomorrow."

"What?" I couldn't imagine who would come out here, much less how he would know.

"Grandma Emma and your dad."

"Oh. How do you know?"

"The spirits told me."

My brow furrowed. "What?"

He chuckled, "I'm kidding. I have a calendar. We set the date for their visit before we came out here. Listen. Grandma Emma and I are going to need some alone time when they get here."

My nose wrinkled for a second, but it gave way to a smile. "You're gross, Grandpa."

He laughed. "I told you before. You won't think so when you're my age."

I just shook my head.

"You need to help me get her alone without making it look like I am trying to get rid of your dad. I don't want to hurt his feelings. And . . . Grandma Emma likes surprises."

He was so ridiculous, I decided just to be a willing accomplice. "What should I do?"

He leaned forward and spoke quickly. Obviously, he had given this a lot of thought.

"So when they get here, I need you to ask Byron to help you check the line. He knows everything about trapping. He grew up in this building for most of his childhood. But he doesn't know where all the sets are, so you can do what we normally do. And if anything strange happens, he'll be there. He probably wants some father-son time anyways."

"I got your back, Grandpa."

"Good boy," he said, clapping me on the shoulder.

Grandpa Liam settled in the rocking chair by the Drolet with Buster in his lap. That's usually where he liked to read. We each had our own kerosene lantern. I started back on my worksheets for Mrs. Byrne's class. It had to be the most boring way to learn and teach. I did homework for about forty-five minutes. When I glanced up, I noticed that Grandpa Liam wasn't reading for once. Tonight he had an old wooden box in his lap next to Buster, and he was holding a photograph. I couldn't see the image from my work station at the kitchen table, but I didn't press him about it. I just kept working until I noticed that he'd fallen asleep in the chair, one hand on the dog, the other still holding that picture.

I rose as quietly as I could and walked over to the chair. Buster was sleeping too. The box was open and seemed to have more pictures and letters, but I couldn't see the front side of the one in his hands. The old man would wake up if I tried to grab it. And it would seem wrong to dig through things when he wasn't looking, so I gently shook his arm.

"Grandpa, do you want to go to bed?"

He seemed slightly startled and sat up in the chair, giving me just a second to see that the photograph was an aged image of three little children in black and white, one girl and two boys. He tucked it into the box and closed the lid.

"Buster, bed time." He stood and went to the sink to brush his teeth.

"Grandpa, who was in that picture?"

"Just ancient memories."

"I like hearing about your memories, Grandpa."

"Not this one. At least, not yet."

There was a strange look on his face, so I let it go. Grandpa Liam and Buster settled into the bunk before I could dig any deeper. More secrets. I didn't even know enough about this one to write it in my notebooks.

WHEN I WOKE UP the next morning, Grandpa was busy. He was sweeping the cabin, scrubbing surfaces, and carefully stacking hides along the south wall. He was humming to himself and glanced at me with smiling eyes. He wore a fresh white tee shirt, clean jeans, and his red suspenders today.

"You just need a disco light for your big date, Grandpa."

He laughed. "I knew we forgot something when we came out here."

I made the oatmeal and washed the dishes, then put on a clean pair of sweat pants, a Minnesota Wild tee shirt, and a bandana. My hair was getting longer and it helped keep the bangs out of my eyes. Buster started to bark. He was not much of a barker or a growler normally, so it seemed strange.

"They're here, Ezra."

As soon as he said that, I heard the whine of a snowmobile cruising in the distance. Within minutes it slowed and downshifted and then approached. Grandpa Liam opened the door and sent Buster out, "Sic 'em, Buster!"

My dad and Grandma Emma were clad in snowmobile suits, hopping off the Backcountry Ski-Doo in an obvious state of excitement. The Backcountry was faster than the Skandic we used for the trapline, but it didn't have as much towing power or a hitch. It was perfect for getting two people from the trailhead to the cabin.

I stepped outside and my dad folded me into a tight embrace, crushing me in his meaty arms. "I missed you, Ezra."

I offered a wan smile as we separated.

"You look older. This winter wind does things to a man's complexion."

"Grandpa's work routine does things to a boy's body too."

My dad's shoulders relaxed and he smiled at me. He looked a little older too, but I didn't say so.

Grandpa and Grandma kissed, as giddy as high school sweethearts. I opened the cabin door for them.

"Grandma Emma, do you want some tea?"

"Look who's all grown up. Yes, Ezra, I'd love some."

I made tea for everyone and we caught up on stories. Grandma Emma and my dad were especially interested in the story of my first kill.

"We'll have to have a feast!" my dad exclaimed earnestly. I knew getting my first moose was a big deal, but it sounded like he expected the whole world come to my feast. "We'll have to do this back on the rez so it's easier for everyone to be there. Maybe we should bring the meat back with us so we can have everything ready when you come back for the Valentine's Day visit."

Grandpa caught my eye and winked.

I rolled my eyes. Of course he'd planned our first trip to the rez to happen on Valentine's Day.

Grandma Emma added, "I will do my finest work for this feast."

Grandpa eyed me expectantly. I was ready.

"Dad, we need to check traps today. Do you want to come with me on the Skandic? The smaller Ski-Doo won't be much use on the line. We can give the old man a break and have a little father-son time."

"Yes, of course!" He seemed energized by the request.

I grabbed the .22 Winchester Magnum Rimfire, a hatchet, two knives, wire, rope, and gunny sacks and put them in the game sled. I gassed up the Ski-doo and waited. It had been weeks but I still felt pangs of anger around my dad, even though I told myself that I shouldn't. I knew in my mind that Grandpa Liam was right. I just couldn't quite bring myself to act that way. I thought about telling him all of this, but the words still seemed to catch in my throat.

He stood by the Skandic to cinch down his hat for the ride. "There's nothing new to report on the Schroeder fire investigation. No arrests, no new inquiries. My guess is, it was just an accident or a problem the Schroeders had with someone we don't know."

I hoped he was right. I nodded back, but I didn't say anything in response. Instead, I told him about Ogimaa and the wolf pack and my rabbit snares. He seemed impressed that my idea worked and even more impressed that Grandpa Liam said that I taught him something. As much as anything, I think he was just grateful that we were having a real conversation.

We ran the south loop without issue. There were a few more beaver sets there, and they always took more time. We motored down the north loop without stopping at the cabin after. We were starting later than usual for checking traps, because we had waited for my dad and Grandma Emma to get to the cabin, so I was a little worried about the time. I was starting to work like Grandpa Liam—fast and confident in routine trap checks and routes. I could tell that my dad was noticing.

When we motored behind Chief's Ridge to check the fisher sets, I had to slow down because some of the cedars hung low over the trail. We had to get off the Ski-Doo to check some of them, but as we approached the final set, only ten yards away, the air sucked deep in my chest and froze. Standing right over our trap was Ogimaa—light gray fur glistening in the winter sun. He was all of his one hundred and seventy-five pounds, muscular and proud, regal and intimidating. Our eyes locked and neither of us moved.

I could feel my dad's presence right behind me.

"Gwis. His front left paw is caught in the trap."

My heart sank. Ogimaa was the most important animal in the forest. He was my friend, my relative.

"Dad, we have to get him out." I could see a little blood by his front left paw. The trap was a 160 Conibear. It was too small to kill a wolf, but it was too big for him to pull free. It wasn't meant for him. Wolves were too clever for traps. This shouldn't be happening.

"Gwis, we might have to use the .22."

"No. No way, Dad. We are wolf clan. It's taboo to kill our own clan."

"I know. But if we leave him there, he'll chew his own leg off and there's no way he'd survive after that. It would be kinder to put him down."

"We can't, Dad. We just can't. I can set him free."

"A wounded animal is nothing to play with, gwis." My dad's voice was firmer now. "He's just as big as you are. He might rip your throat out—not out of malice, but fear."

My dad might have been right, but I couldn't listen. I stepped forward. Ogimaa's ears flattened on his head, and a low, slow growl rumbled from his throat.

"Gwis!" My dad's voice was laced with fear now. But he was too far behind to restrain me.

I stepped forward again and again. I was focused now on Ogimaa: the angle of his neck, the most likely response if I grabbed him.

My dad was hollering, "Gwis, don't you dare!"

I lunged forward with all the strength in my legs and collided with Ogimaa. I was just fast enough to avoid the first snap of his teeth. He might have been stronger than me, and he might have been faster. But I had watched a lot more UFC. I was reckless and foolish. I could have been killed or hurt or given my dad a heart attack. But Royce Gracie would have been proud.

I wrapped both of my arms around Ogimaa's neck and both of my legs around his belly. He was so strong, writhing in my grasp and snapping his head side to side. If I released him even one inch, he'd have enough room to sink his canines into my shoulder. He was growling and barking at the same time with a ferocity and volume that sounded like a horror movie. That alone nearly made me let go and try to run. But my best chance now was to hang on and squeeze.

"Dad! Release the trap!"

I held on to Ogimaa with all the strength in my body. My dad ran up and squeezed the tensioner springs on the trap in his big, brown hands. Ogimaa gave a primal growl and snapped at my dad's arms, just inches from his muzzle. But I held fast. I heard the metallic squeal of the springs and then Ogimaa's paw popped free. I relaxed my legs and arms and Ogimaa sprang forth with athletic fury, bounding through the snow and brush. In a flash, he was gone.

I sat up, catching my breath, eye-to-eye with my father for a long, pregnant silence. I knew that he wanted to admonish me for being such a foolish child. But I think part of him maybe admired me too for being such a foolish man. After several minutes, he just stood up and offered his hand to help pull me to my feet.

Chapter 20

THE WIND RUSHED, whistled, and whipped at my parka as I opened the throttle on the Ski-Doo, cutting straight through the narrows by Bear Pass on Rainy Lake. Buster gave up on trying to see and hunkered down inside my coat. Grandpa Liam held on to my waist. I probably made a good wind blocker for him. Once we made it through the pass, Red Gut Bay opened up and we saw signs of civilization, however fleeting, as we powered across the ice. Houses appeared every few miles until finally we saw the landing, fish houses, and track homes of the rez at Red Gut, proudly announced by the Nigigoonsiminikaaning First Nation sign.

We made the entire trip by snowmobile in record time. We didn't need the game sled or any supplies because we had already sent all of my first kill ahead with Grandma Emma and Dad. It hadn't snowed in two weeks, and the sun had worked the accumulated snow into a hard pack on the ice. Grandpa Liam didn't even complain about my driving. Even though Grandma had just come to the cabin a couple weeks ago, I think Grandpa Liam was still excited to be reunited with her.

We planned to stay at Red Gut for two days. The traps were still out at Chief's Ridge. It was Friday and I had to email all my homework to my teachers, get new assignments, and meet with instructors over Zoom before the weekend. Grandpa Liam wanted to spend time with Grandma Emma. My dad would be back on the rez in the evening, and tomorrow would be my big first kill feast. I had never even been to one before.

The first thing I did was plug in my smartphone and turn it on. I knew there would be updates from Noah, Oliver, and Amelia, and of course, I wanted to see if there were any messages from Nora. It started to ping relentlessly as soon as it powered on. Daniel Drumbeater had left one just to check up on me. Noah and Oliver said there was no sign of Matt and that the investigation was still open, but nobody had been to the school since. Things were, for the most part, going back to normal. I had missed the latest release of *Call of Duty* though.

There were as many messages from Nora as there were from everyone else combined. She had given me a blow-by-blow description of everything happening in Northeast, knowing I wouldn't see it until now. It seemed like Matt Schroeder was still staying in Milwaukee. Nora had done her interview finally. Like Noah and Oliver, she'd heard the investigation was still open, but other than her interview, she hadn't heard anything new. I had to turn in my homework and meet my teachers on Zoom first, but then I planned to give her a call to catch up.

I had actually stayed on top of my schoolwork, so connecting with my teachers and turning everything in was easy enough. My dad had left his laptop with Grandma Emma so I'd have everything I needed. It was the first time I'd seen Mr. Lukas since I punched the locker. I'd thought it would be more awkward than it was.

It was funny seeing my teachers' names displayed on the Zoom screen—Josef Lukas, Fiona Byrne. I wasn't used to seeing their first names. It made me think about how people usually emphasized age, position, and power in mainstream society, like respect could be commanded by a title or name formalities instead of earned. I respected my teachers, but not because someone made me call them by their last names all the time.

I texted Nora after that and tried to call, but there was no response. I hoped she was okay. There was nothing to do but wait.

Grandma Emma was wearing a blue dress, red shirt, and blue calico apron as usual. She made great heaping plates of spaghetti for me and Grandpa Liam. I took a hot shower after that, and the warm current coursing over my body felt so divine I wondered if should make a tobacco offering in sincere appreciation. My heart was at Chief's Ridge now, but cleaning up with a wash basin at the cabin was no comparison to this.

We sat on the couch after doing the dishes to watch *Powwow Highway*. Grandpa Liam slapped his knees, rocking back and forth with laughter when Philbert, played by Gary Farmer, stood naked by the bed to wake up Buddy. As was tradition, Grandpa's laughing got Buster barking and pretty soon Grandma Emma and I were laughing right along with him. Grandpa and Grandma went to bed after that, and I sat on the couch with Buster to watch the latest episodes of *Boruto* and then UFC fight highlights until my dad came back. Royce Gracie was famous for his submission holds, but it was cool to see the spotlight they did on his takedowns too.

The next morning was a flurry of activity. Grandma Emma had moose roasts in the oven, wild rice on the stove, and hominy soup with moose meat in a crock pot.

She had a list of jobs too, and started barking orders in her calico apron so Grandpa, Dad, and I jumped up and got to it. I was slicing backstraps and frying them. My dad and Grandpa Liam brought the first items of food to the community center for the feast. They came back for Grandma and me and the rest of the food. Buster had to wait this one out. Dogs were forbidden to attend ceremonies.

"Why can't Buster come?"

"You tell him, Byron."

"Okay. Sit down, gwis. This won't take long." Dad motioned to the kitchen chair opposite him.

He seemed hesitant for a second, maybe unsure if I wanted to get this from him, but he looked at me intently as he sat on the other side of the table.

"Do you remember who Nenabozho is, gwis?"

"Yeah. He's half human, half spirit."

"Right," he continued. "When earth was new, he traveled the whole earth with the wolf. They named all things in creation. And when they were done, the Great Spirit told them that he was pleased. Now they had to part company. They could not live or travel together anymore, but they would have parallel lives. What happened to one would happen to the other. And this is how it has been ever since. The wolf nation and our people both were misunderstood, feared, and subjected to genocide by strangers from across the ocean. But both stayed true to their paths, remained spiritually strong, overcame adversity, hid from enemies, took care of their people, regrew their nations, and today are healing and making a comeback. Since dogs are cousins of the wolves, we keep them away from ceremonies to honor our original instructions."

He gave me a nod and rose from the chair. I caught Grandma Emma nodding approval on the other side of the kitchen when I stood to finish getting ready.

Grandma Emma handed me a ribbon shirt—dark blue like the night sky, with silver ribbons and a wolf emblem on the back embroidered in silver thread with black and brown highlights. "Put this on, Ezra. We have to get to the feast."

"Thanks, Grandma."

"You're welcome. It has a wolf on there for your clan, and silver for the stars in the night sky for your name, Anangoowinini."

"It's awesome."

She smiled.

I slipped on the ribbon shirt and ran a comb through my hair. I could feel my heartbeat quicken in anticipation of the feast as we put the rest of the pots of cooked food in the truck and then took boxes of the carefully packaged moose meat to fill the back of the Silverado.

My dad and Grandma Emma had spent two days processing the moose quarters and other cuts into neat, sealed, two-pound FoodSaver vacuum-sealed bags.

"There is so much food. Who's coming to this feast?" I asked.

Grandma Emma smiled knowingly. "Ezra, my dear, everyone is coming to your feast."

Chapter 21

I WAS SHOCKED WHEN we got to the community center to see the parking lot full of cars. I glanced at my dad and grandparents, but they were quiet. We walked through the door and it was even more crowded than I thought. I didn't even know some of the people. The bleachers were pulled out and I noticed many of the tribal elders sitting in the front. They were laughing and visiting loudly. Daniel Drumbeater was telling a story to several of them, and it must have been good because they were all cackling. I could tell that some of our cousins from Couchiching and Seine River were there too. There were kids everywhere, running in circles on the gym floor and playing tag.

My cousin Elroy Dubois came over. He was my age, but with a classical Ojibwe build, broad-shouldered but short in the legs. He held out his hand, offering a formal handshake, and said, "Congratulations, cuz."

I grabbed his hand and pulled him in to a bro-hug. "I had no idea so many people would be here."

"Yeah, it's a big deal." Elroy wasn't much of a talker, but he didn't walk away. I think he was genuinely proud of me. I felt a subtle swell of energy running through me and around the room.

Elroy's sister, Dora, came over too. She was a few years younger than Elroy, but their resemblance was unmistakable. "I heard you shot a big moose, Ezra." She was so cute, her eyes as big as maple sugar cakes and words that seemed to tumble out in slow motion. She just looked up at me when I gave her a hug.

"Yeah," I said. "His horns were this big." I spread my arms out to show the width of the moose rack, exaggerating their girth and intentionally giving Elroy a gentle smack in the chest. Both of them started to laugh. We chatted about fishing for a couple of minutes, but more and more people kept coming up to me.

My cousin Stanley sauntered up next. He had survived that short stay in Northeast Minneapolis years ago, but stayed on the rez since then. He was my dad's age.

"Ez, congratulations on your first kill. I agreed to help get everything set up. Give me a hand with the tables and chairs."

"Of course." I was glad to have something to do.

We placed numerous tables with chairs around them in front of the bleachers. Then we laid out food mats in a neat line on the floor from east to west to receive Grandma Emma's culinary genius.

Stanley and my dad gathered a couple of my other cousins and together we went back to the truck, hauling all the frozen moose meat in and placing it on the food mats next to all the pots and roasting pans Grandma Emma had been preparing, and all the other cooked food. Now I was starting to feel nervous.

My dad placed a chair for me right at the east end of the food mats and then he pulled up a chair and sat next to me. Grandpa Liam and Grandma Emma sat next to him on the south side, starting a circle around the food. As soon as they sat, about twenty men stood up and worked their way through the bleachers and chairs to the food, carrying their own chairs. They sat next to my grandparents one at a time.

I hadn't seen Daniel Drumbeater since Nora and I bumped into him at his fish house, when we saw the wolves chasing deer on the lake. He wasn't chief of Nigigoonsiminikaaning First Nation when my parents asked him to be my namesake, but it made me feel a little conspicuous that he was chief now. In addition to their other duties, it was a special right and obligation of namesakes to support their charges at ceremonies like this. He looked down the line of people seated and caught my eye. Then he winked and sat back in his chair.

The tribal elders and community members moved up close and we were eventually surrounded by rings of people in a large circle with the food in the middle. Everyone was looking at me. It was then that I noticed Nora George sitting by Ruth George and Rita Kingfisher at the west end of the circle. I could feel my heart rate accelerating as Nora gave me a shy smile and a little wave, her fingers extending beyond the sleeves of a pink running shirt.

My dad leaned over to me and whispered in my ear, "Ezra, when I offer you the food, you have to refuse the first three times." Then he gave me detailed instructions about what to say and do after that.

My cousin Stanley took a birchbark bowl full of tobacco and slowly walked around the room, giving some to each person in attendance, including the kids. Grandpa Liam stood up and spoke briefly in Ojibwe: "Indinawemaaganidog, odaapinaadaa wa'aw asemaa! Oshkinitaage Anangoowinini."

It was customary to build a fire in the stone ring outside the door of the community center when there was a ceremony in progress. Many people took their tobacco outside and put it in the fire. Others lit pipes and sat inside the center, smoking. It took several minutes, but when everyone had settled back into their places, Grandpa Liam stood and started to speak again.

"Indinawemaaganidog, onjida gigiiwitaabimin. Ani-ininiiwi noozhishenh." This time he spoke for a long time, talking to our Creator and the spirits in the four winds, the water, and woods. He mentioned the animals, birds, and fish, Nenabozho, the sun, moon, and stars. He told the people how grateful our family was to welcome me to the ranks of hunters sitting next to him. Then he turned to me and told me to tell the story of my kill.

This was my first time speaking in public except for a couple of minor school classroom presentations. I stumbled and bumbled my way through it, but people were laughing when I explained about Grandpa Liam taking a nap rather than coaching me through my shot. I could see the men nodding approval when I finished the story.

My dad uncovered one of the pots, used a spoon to grab a morsel of moose meat, kneeled in front of my chair, and held it up to my mouth.

"Gwis."

"Gaawiin. Indinenimaag abinoojiinyag ayaanzigwaa gegoo ji-miijiwaad. No," I said, following his instructions, "I'm thinking of children who don't have enough to eat."

There were a few murmurs and nods among the men sitting next to Grandpa Liam.

"Gwis."

"Gaawiin. Indinenimaag gichi-aya'aag gashkitoosigwaa ji-bami'idizowaad. No. I'm thinking of my elders who can't get out in the woods to hunt for themselves."

There was more nodding, and I could feel all eyes on me as my dad pulled the spoon back and offered it to me a third time.

"Gwis."

"Gaawiin. Indinenimaag indinaawemaaganag, niijanishinaabeg, miinawaa gaa-pi-izhaajig ji-wiidookawiwaad. No. I'm thinking of my family, my community, and people who came here today to support me."

He pulled the spoon back and then offered it to me a fourth time. "Gwis." He nodded, and I opened my mouth and took the meat, chewing slowly and aware of every set of eyes in the building still fixed on me. My dad returned to his seat and Grandpa Liam started to speak again.

"Ezra, you just changed your life. Up until today, you were what we called a dependent. You depended on all of the people in this room to provide all of your food." My gaze shifted around the room from Daniel Drumbeater to the George family to my grandparents and my dad. Grandpa Liam continued, "But today, you are providing for all of us. This is what it means to be an adult. From today on, you will have a special power. It's the power to gather resources. You'll have it when you hunt and trap, when you fish, when you pick berries, and when you get a job. Use your power to think of children in need, elders who can't get it for themselves, your family and community."

My dad leaned over and whispered to me: "You have to get up now. Open the first box of moose meat and start giving packages to everyone in the circle. Come back for more when the box is empty and keep giving it away until there is nothing left. Move clockwise."

I did what I was told. I grabbed several packages of meat from the first box and circled around the feast to the start of the line, handing them to Daniel Drumbeater and the other men sitting next to him. Daniel smiled when I handed him a large backstrap. "Gidishpenimin, we'! I'm proud of you."

Stanley slapped me on the arm when I gifted some to him. "Miigwech!"

It was a strange feeling, giving away my kill. The elders seemed so happy to receive packages of meat. Many people shook my hand. I felt like I mattered in a way I had never felt before. Something was stirring inside of me and I knew that if I had anything else to give, I would gladly do so.

It took me twenty minutes to finish circling the people and giving away my kill. When I sat back down, Grandpa Liam invited all the other successful hunters to share teachings with me. Some of them spoke for a long time.

Daniel Drumbeater said: "Ezra, you'll notice many different kinds of moose in the woods—calves, cows, young bulls, and big, mature bulls with a large rack of horns. Moose can be dangerous. They are usually happy to eat lily pad roots and be left alone, but on the rare occasions when one attacks a human, it is not usually a big, mature, fully antlered male that charges. The most likely moose to charge a person is a young bull. And that's the moose that's most likely to be shot or hit by a car. You see, Ezra, the moose is a metaphor for manhood. We often make our biggest mistakes when we are young. That's when we're more likely to drive too fast and pay the price, to experiment with alcohol and drugs, to go on a date and not respect our partner, or to hurt ourselves. If you want to live to be a big, mature, fully antlered bull, you have to act like one. You have to move a little slower and think before you act."

That hit me in a way that all the books and lessons at school never could. I made a silent vow to move a little slower and think before I acted. I would listen to my elders, and I'd protect them too.

After they were done, the men stood and came to shake my hand. Many of them gave me gifts—skinning knives, a flint and steel, pouches of tobacco, a new set of gloves, a flannel shirt, and more. We started the feast immediately after that. I helped my cousins make plates for the elders and most of them moved to the tables in front of the bleachers to eat. Everyone wanted to talk to me, to ask about school, when I'd get my driver's license, how I liked working on the trapline.

I hadn't realized until then how much the members of my community watched me and cared about me. I wanted to make them proud. I found myself wishing that my mom was here to see this. I wanted to make her proud too.

Chapter 22

WHEN EVERYONE WAS DONE eating at the center, we sent the few leftovers from the feast home with elders from the community and spent another hour cleaning up. I helped bring the pots back to Grandpa and Grandma's to wash everything up.

I took another long, hot shower after that. I stood in the bathroom, looking at myself in the mirror. I could tell that running trapline was changing my body: my neck, shoulders, and arms were getting bigger. My hair was getting longer. It was almost long enough for a ponytail now. I decided that I wouldn't cut it anymore. I'd grow it back out into a long powwow braid again. And I'd have to start shaving sometime in the coming months or I'd soon be sporting a mustache like Pedro in *Napoleon Dynamite*.

I opened up the medicine cabinet to see if there was any shaving stuff in there, but the first thing I noticed was a bottle of silver sulfadiazine with a prescription label for Emma Cloud. I picked it up and read the directions and details. It was for treating second- and third-degree burns. I checked the date of the prescription: November 30. Grandpa Liam was telling the truth. Grandma Emma must have burned her hand weeks before the Schroeder fire.

I got dressed quickly after that, slipping into jeans and insulated muck boots with a clean tee shirt and my school jacket, gray, puffy, and clean. I stuffed the red notebook with my musings on the Schroeder fire inside, slipped on my winter clothes, and walked over to Nora's. I was so overwhelmed with the people at the feast that I didn't get a chance to connect with her. The sun was setting by the time I got to Rita's, but the temperature was uncommonly warm for February and I could tell we were going to get snow. I knocked on the door and Nora answered.

"Hey," I said. "I had no idea you'd be here for the feast. I'm dying to hear what you've learned about the Schroeder investigation! Should we walk and talk?"

"Yes, wait right here."

It seemed a little weird to have me wait outside, but it didn't take long for her to emerge. I never watched the Maple Leafs, to be honest, but given how their gear looked on Nora, they were my favorite hockey team by far.

Nora was leaning forward and animated as we started walking. "Ez! Your feast! That was amazing. I am so proud of you. I was kind of surprised, honestly, to hear that my mom wanted to drive all the way back here for a feast, but now I know why. You must be having the most amazing experience with your Grandpa Liam."

"Thanks." I guess I was having an amazing experience with Grandpa Liam. But it was more than that. I just didn't have words for all of it. "I'm learning a lot."

She looped her mittened hand around my bicep for a second and looked at me. "I can tell. You look different."

"I do?"

"Yeah. In a good way."

Maybe she could tell that my arms were getting bigger. I smiled. "Nora, I didn't get all your texts until yesterday. I tried to call."

"I know. We were on our way here and it would have been awkward to catch up on the investigation in the car with my mom. You go first."

"I have a little information on the Schroeder fire, but you probably learned more than me."

"What do you know?"

"Well, my dad was with me all night on the night of the fire. I had heavy pain medication and wouldn't have been able to make it over there. He stayed with me, I think he was worried about my injury from punching the locker and some crazy talk I threw at him that day. I don't think it could have been either one of us."

"But we knew that, didn't we?"

"I guess I still had a few doubts, but they're put to rest now. And my Grandma Emma has a burn on her hand."

"What?"

"Yeah. That's what I thought. I found out both of my grandparents came to Northeast on the night of the fire."

"No way. I've never seen them there!"

"It all seemed super suspicious, and none of the adults here want to tell me everything they know. But Grandpa Liam said that Grandma Emma burned her hand on a bannock pan at the end of November and tonight I saw the burn cream prescription with her name on it. It was dated November 30. I think that story checks out. I wrote down everything I could think of in the notebook you gave me. I'll leave it with you in case you can connect some of the dots that I just can't see."

I unslung my backpack and rummaged around for the red notebook and handed it to her.

"Ezra, I found out a few things too."

"What do you know?"

"Well, Detective Williams still has an open investigation. They aren't sharing information with high school kids. Or their parents. But they still haven't arrested anyone or named anyone as a suspect."

"I know, my dad told me. I bet it was some criminal the Schroeders were selling their drugs to."

"Maybe you're right. But Ezra . . . I did an internet search on Mark and Luke Schroeder too. All criminal convictions are public record." We were all alone on the loop road, so it seemed strange when her voice dropped to a murmur. "Luke was convicted of manslaughter ten years ago and went to prison for over five years. Mark had three assault convictions."

"They're gone now. They can't hurt us."

She gave me a wan smile. "Thanks for the reassurance. It's just been stressful."

"It'll be okay, Nora." I gave her a quick hug.

"My mom has been driving me to school just to be safe. And I go to the Boys & Girls Club until she's done with work, then she drives me back to the house. But I don't want to live like that forever."

"Well, it can't take them that long to finish the investigation, and then this whole thing will be behind us. And at least Matt won't be coming to Canada. I doubt he even has a passport."

"Customs and immigration won't let him cross. But Ezra, the US-Canadian border is the longest unprotected international border in the world. He could just stroll onto Rainy Lake on the US side and walk right over on the ice. Nobody would even see him do it!"

"We're just a few hundred yards away if that ever happens."

"When you're not on the trapline."

I didn't really have an answer for that. I sighed. "I wish you could stay here until the whole investigation was over."

"Me too. I didn't ask, though. I think my mom would have a really hard time if we spent that much time apart."

I saw a chunk of brown ice on the road. It seemed so out of place—it must have fallen off one of the cars coming into the housing tract. I kicked at it nervously.

"Nora, I have another question. Tomorrow is Valentine's Day. Grandpa Liam is a hopeless romantic. My dad will be heading back to Minneapolis. We're not heading back to the trapline until Monday morning. I know Grandpa Liam will want me to leave the house so he and Grandma Emma can be alone."

"That's cute."

"They're gross, actually."

Nora laughed.

"But they are cute," I conceded.

"So?"

It was a little more work to muster the courage for my next question, but I felt emboldened by everything that had happened at the feast. I kicked the ice chunk a little farther down the road and it went skidding across the smooth surface and out of reach.

"So, I was wondering if you wanted to hang out together tomorrow? Maybe we could go for a snowmobile ride or something."

"Sure."

We headed back to Rita Kingfisher's house after that. I knew that Nora only saw me as a close friend, but I had just arranged a Valentine's Day date with her: I was feeling pretty great.

Nora seemed energized too. "Charlotte and Amelia and I joined curling!"

"Curling? Isn't that an old man sport?"

She laughed. "No. It's a cool person sport, and it's way more fun than bowling. We have room for a fourth person on our squad if you ever decide to come back to civilization."

I had an image of Nora slinging curling stones while Amelia and Charlotte worked lead and second, sweeping the rink ice ahead of her stone. How sweet it would be to watch her laugh and smile and look at me. "Yeah, Nora. I'd like that."

We were at Rita's driveway by then, so I gave her quick hug and turned back to head for Grandpa and Grandma's house. There was just a faint hint of perfume in the air.

It was starting to snow by the time I made it back. I had told Grandpa Liam that I was planning to be gone for the day after my dad left. He'd put his arm up to give me a fist bump. I shook my head. He could even make a fist bump uncool. I had just bumped him back so he'd quit.

I walked over to the television to see if it was new enough to have Bluetooth. "Grandpa Liam, I love watching old Indian movies with you. But do you want to try something new?"

"Is it a Native movie?"

"It is. Give me just a minute."

I connected my smartphone to his television Bluetooth and opened my Hulu app. "This one is called *Reservation Dogs*."

"I like the sound of that."

Grandpa Liam was in true form. He laughed even harder than usual, because unlike his favorite Native films, he had actually never seen this one before. And the punky Native kids could have come straight out of Red Gut. We finished two episodes.

"You mean there's more?"

"Yeah. There are three full seasons—twenty-eight episodes."

"Praise to the Manidoog! Emma, we gotta get Hulu."

I was pretty pleased with myself after that. I admit that the old man was showing me a lot of new stuff, but I was teaching him too.

In the morning, Grandma Emma was cooking up a storm and my cell phone buzzed with new text messages. It was all Nora. She wanted to make plans.

Ezra, see if your dad can give us a ride to International Falls on his way to Minneapolis.

You wanna hang out there today?

Let's watch a movie at the Cine 5.

Okay.

Then we can walk across the bridge to Fort Frances and get some food on the Canadian side.

Sounds great.

My mom can pick us up there and bring us back to the rez.

Nice.

She's taking the day off tomorrow and we'll go back to Minneapolis on Monday.

Perfect.

This was going to be the best Valentine's Day ever. I did my best to appear self-sacrificing with all the adults.

As always, my dad was hunched over his computer trying to answer emails. "Dad, I thought it would be nice to give Grandpa and Grandma some time alone today. Could you give Nora and me a ride to International Falls to watch a movie? We'll walk back across the bridge to the Fort and then Ruth can pick us up in Fort Frances and bring us back to the rez."

"Fantastic idea," Grandpa Liam said without hesitation.

My dad just smiled and answered, "Sure, son."

"And Dad, can I have some money for the movie and food?"

Grandma Emma chuckled. My dad and Grandpa Liam reached for their wallets at the same time. This was going even better than I expected.

"We can go in a few hours, gwis."

It took me a lot longer than I expected to figure out what to wear. I had never been on a real date before, even if it was just a date between friends. I washed my puffer jacket and a load of clothes and showered. I chose my black Vans, jeans, and a green hoodie. It was a relaxed look, but the hoodie made my shoulders look big.

"Lookin' fresh, grandson." Grandpa Liam winked at me when I was ready.

"She's just a friend, Grandpa."

"I know. A very cute fr—"

"Quit! Grandpa, that joke was old already during the Great Depression."

He just laughed.

Ugh. I still had an hour before we were supposed to leave. I was nervous and didn't know what to do with myself, so I figured I better quit thinking about the date and distract myself with some writing. I grabbed my notebook and went in the bathroom for some privacy to write about the first kill feast and my date with Nora. I sat on the stool and opened it up.

My stomach turned and my heart leapt up into my throat. *I was looking at the journal with all my notes on the Schroeder fire.* Last night, I'd given Nora the wrong notebook. She had the one with all my secrets—Matt Schroeder's hazing of me at summer camp, all my memories of my mom, and every single detail of my feelings for her. I was totally exposed.

Chapter 23

MY HANDS SHOOK AS my long, brown fingers tried to tap out a message to Nora. How could I be so stupid? She'd never talk to me again. Man, my hands were as clumsy as my dad's. It took me three tries and restarts with the predictive text prompts running wild from my mistyping.

Nora, please don't look at the notebook I gave you last night. I gave you the wrong one by accident. That one was more of a journal. It was just meant for me.

I felt like I might puke waiting for her response. I saw the three dots, then . . .

I'm sorry, Ezra. I read the whole thing last night. I thought you wanted me to.

Oh my God. What should I do?

Nora messaged again, *Are you mad at me?*

No. How could I be mad at her? I was mad at myself.

Can we still go to the movie?

Yeah. Of course.

I guess I'd just have to face the music.

The ride from Red Gut to International Falls was super awkward. I sat in the back so Nora wouldn't have to sit there alone. She handed me my notebook as soon as she got in the car and I hurriedly stuffed it in my backpack. But she didn't look at me right away. I had no idea what to say, so there were a few minutes of nervous silence.

Nora had her white winter coat and tight jeans on, with her white high tops. I realized she weirdly seemed in good spirits. I was the one feeling a little sick to my stomach. It was hard to shake. Nora ignored my awkwardness and engaged my dad in chitchat throughout the ride.

We made our way across the Noden Causeway, back through Fort Frances, and across the bridge to International Falls. Since the Falls was on the US side of the border, I flashed with worry for a minute that Matt Schroeder might get to us there, even though I knew I was just being paranoid. There was no way for him to know where we'd be. The Cine 5 was a tiny theater, but we were safe.

I bought tickets for the movie.

"I can pay my own way, Ezra."

"My treat today." My voice sounded sheepish.

"Okay. Thanks, Ez."

We stood in awkward silence until we got popcorn, candy, and drinks and then shuffled into the theater. I still didn't know how to feel around Nora and I didn't know how to get a conversation started. It would seem too heavy to talk about the journal, and it would seem superficial if I tried to make small talk. I kept glancing at her to see if it was even half as awkward for her, but she was fine. I probably seemed as jittery as a red squirrel, trying to remember where he stashed all the pinecones. But once we settled into our seats, Nora turned to me and whispered in my ear, "You don't have to say a single word, but I want you to know that I loved everything you wrote in your journal." Then she took her hand from my ear and laced her fingers in mine as the previews started.

I was so glad she had one of those running shirts on where just your fingers and thumb stick out, because my palms were sweaty for the entire show. At least it would be hard for her to tell how bad it was. But I knew that something was happening between us. I was more than a friend now.

After the movie, as we exited the Cine 5, I saw someone run across the road wearing a baseball hat with a greasy blond mullet protruding from the back. It felt like my heart dropped from chest to my guts for a second. Had Matt Schroeder made it to International Falls? But the guy turned up the street and disappeared into one of the stores a minute later. Matt would have challenged us for sure if he was there. My mind was playing tricks on me.

Nora seemed radiant as we strolled down the snow-covered sidewalks in International Falls, past the Kerry Park Arena and over the international bridge. Packaging Corporation of America was keeping up their daily routine, dumping chemicals in the Rainy River, enveloping the town in rancid odor. But Nora was chatting away and smiling and even PCA couldn't sour my mood. In Fort Frances, we poked around the stores and went to the Flint House for supper. Supper cost fifty dollars, and even in Canadian funds, it seemed like a lot to me. My dad must have spent a fortune feeding me over the years.

Nora's eyes were dancing as we talked and talked. "Ezra, we don't have to talk about what's in your notebook if you don't want to. But I would never share anything you put in there with anyone else."

"Thanks. Yeah, just keep it between us."

"Of course."

"I guess I'm glad that you know everything now. I was embarrassed about some of it."

"There's nothing to be embarrassed about, Ez. Matt Schroeder was so awful to you. Talking about it might help. And everything that you've been through, losing your mom? I'm really sorry. And I'm here for you."

I dared a deeper look into her eyes and felt something stirring inside me. I just couldn't tell if it might be a laugh, a cry, or a lot of vomit. I managed a wan smile, and she reached across the table to hold my hand for a minute. She never looked away.

"I think I felt ashamed of not sticking up for myself better with Matt. And I felt like my dad could have stopped my mom from working at that pulp mill . . . like her life wasn't worth protecting. We could have moved somewhere else. I felt like he didn't protect her. But she . . . she didn't protect herself either. I've just been so mad about everything. She should still be here."

"Ezra, I hope you know that you've done a great job of standing up to Matt. And your dad and mom have done the best they could. Your mom wanted to live. Your dad wanted to spend the rest of his life with her. Maybe they were just doing the best they could?"

"Part of me knows that. But it's been really hard to feel that."

"You're worth sticking up for and sticking around for, Ezra."

"Thanks." I was fiddling with my plate now, trying not to look at her.

"Ezra, my dad died when I was a little girl. I know it's not the same as what you're going through with your mom. But I lost someone really important too."

"I know." I moved the empty plate in a slow circle on the table.

"I got mad at him for not being careful enough on the ice. I got mad at my mom for not stopping him. I even got mad at the Great Spirit for letting it happen. But it got better when I talked about it. My Grandma Rita gave me a reality check. You can talk to me any time, Ez."

That was all I could handle on that topic, and Nora seemed to intuit the need for a change of subject. She launched into a long share about her powwow regalia. She was beading a new belt for her jingle dress and planning to sew copper jingles in place of the silver ones. Thinking about her wearing that lifted my spirits. I didn't have much to contribute on jingle dresses, but I was happy to listen.

Ruth was a little late picking us up, but I didn't mind a bit. Nora still seemed light and energized and full of chatter. When Ruth's Toyota Highlander pulled up by the Flint House, I started to get a little nervous about how this date would end. We sat together in the back seat again on the way back to the rez.

"Sorry I'm late," Ruth said. Her eyes radiated kindness and intelligence through the rearview mirror. "How was dinner?"

"Flint House has perfected Ontario comfort food." Nora beamed.

"That's good."

I felt a little awkward worrying that Ruth might figure out that Nora and I could be more than friends, but Nora was unperturbed.

"Mom, do you know if there's a decent curling rink in Fort Frances? Ezra wants to sling rocks."

"Is that so? Well, the Fort Frances Curling Club is probably the only place in town, but they're only open to the public one or two nights per week." Ruth seemed calm and reserved, driving like it was another afternoon commute in Northeast Minneapolis, her thin leather gloves holding the wheel at ten-and-two and eyes on the road.

"Ezra," she said, "that was a beautiful ceremony yesterday. Congratulations."

"Thanks."

"You're turning into a fine young man."

Nora smiled. I looked out the window to feign interest in the trees whizzing by in the dark.

Ruth still kept her eyes on the road, but I could see the faint outlines of a smile through the rearview mirror.

Ruth navigated to Rita's, parked, and got out. She leaned back in for just a second. "Good night, you two." Then she shut the car door and went inside without even looking back. We got out of the car. Nora waited until she was inside and then turned to me.

"Thank you for the best Valentine's Day ever, Ezra."

"I had a great time." There was a pause in the conversation as I searched for the right words. "Nora . . ." I started.

"Shhhh," she replied, putting a finger to my lips.

Then, before I could respond, she pulled her finger away, leaned in, and put her lips right where her finger had been. A strange tingle started there at the front of my mouth, nose, and cheeks, and coursed through my entire body. All I could do was kiss her back.

We separated and opened our eyes, holding each other's gaze for a few seconds. Not wanting to spoil the moment, I gave her a smile and turned to start the walk back to Grandpa Liam and Grandma Emma's, but I tangled up my feet in the effort and nearly fell. Nora started to bubble with laughter and I looked back over my shoulder, grinning and giggling along with her, marveling all the while at her fine brown face and her smile, as pure and profound as the winter snow.

Chapter 24

THERE ARE THIRTEEN lunar cycles each year, and the Ojibwe calendar marks all thirteen cycles, rather than the twelve months of the Gregorian calendar much of the world uses today. March holds the intersection of two cycles that start the transition to spring, our season of new life and renewal. The Ojibwe lunar cycles that intersect in March are Bebookwaagime-giizis and Onaabani-giizis. These are the moons when the snow starts to melt and then freeze. It's also one of the snowiest times of the year. Some people call the last one Aandego-giizis because the crows mark the beginning of the great bird migrations back to the northland. When those lunar cycles ended, Grandpa Liam always pulled traps.

With the weather starting to warm up a little, the animals moved around more. That made it prime time for trapping. By the end of the season, some of the creeks and rivers had more open spots, and the muskrats had predictable places and paths. Grandpa Liam was thrilled with our success this year.

Grandpa Liam and I were in sync with every aspect of our trapping routine. Every other weekend, Grandma Emma or my dad would drive to the logging skid zone and we'd haul our hides to the truck with the Skandic, so they could be piled up in Grandpa's porch on the rez. When we'd started the trapping season, I wanted nothing more than to be out in the woods as much as possible, but now I liked the weekend trips back to the rez. I had service for my smartphone, and Nora really liked to text.

Ruth and Nora even came back to Red Gut one weekend. Ruth was trying to get Nora breaks from Northeast when she could. Nora came to Grandpa Liam and Grandma Emma's for movies one night. We watched more *Reservation Dogs* and she giggled nonstop at Buster and Grandpa Liam's television antics.

For our last trip to Chief's Ridge, Grandpa Liam and I got to the cabin right at sunset. We planned a couple more weeks trapping before we pulled our sets and closed up for the season. In the fading golden light, we could see footprints all over the yard in front of the cabin and up to the shed. They were smaller than a wolf, fox, or coyote, but I couldn't be sure what they were.

Grandpa Liam gestured with his mitten. "Ezra, they're fisher tracks. All over. They must be scavenging. I bet there's enough residual scent from our previous kills in the shed to keep them poking around. We'll have to be extra careful with our food and hide caching. And we should set a couple sets right on the wall of the shed itself. If they get brave enough to come raiding, we'll be ready. You make the sets."

I nodded and bought our supplies in the cabin. Then I spent thirty minutes tacking up fisher sets. I had to finish up with a flashlight in the fading light. I noticed a strong odor coming from the shed, acrid and penetrating. It smelled kind of like skunk, but distinct and oddly stronger.

When I came in, Grandpa Liam was working on supper over the Drolet in his suspenders and Dickies.

"What's that weird smell in the shed? Did you notice it?"

He laughed. "That's those fishers. They have one of the strongest scent glands in the entire forest. They must have been spraying around in the shed. Once they spray something down, no other predator will touch it. That's how they protect their kills from wolves and bears."

Since we were just back from the rez, Grandpa Liam had fresh pork chops and potatoes for supper. It was a quick pleasure to finish that off. I read *Tracks* by Louise Erdrich for a while. The tales of Eli and Nector somehow reminded me of Grandpa Liam.

In the morning I woke first for a change, eager to check my fisher sets. I stoked the coals in the Drolet, added a couple logs, then slipped on my muck boots and a jacket and went outside. The first hints of dawn were in the sky, but it was still pretty dark and the overcast sky blunted the first light. But I could see a dark shape where I made the first fisher set on the side of the shed. I strode up quickly, excited at the prospect of a successful kill.

Then came a blood-curdling scream from the shed. There is no way to properly describe that sound. It was supernatural—like the worst witch sound in *The Conjuring* or *The Blair Witch Project*, only louder. I whipped around faster than a lynx on a snowshoe hare and bolted for the cabin, casting one terrified glance over my shoulder, just in time to see a large fisher charging straight at me. An adult fisher can easily weigh fifteen pounds, but they grow to three feet in length and look much larger in their winter fur—especially when they charge you before you even had a chance to pee first thing in the morning.

His first bite caught my jacket from the back before I could get to the cabin door. I could feel him pulling and shaking his head, hissing through clenched teeth. The animal was utterly fearless.

The cabin door sprang open and Grandpa Liam whirled around me in long johns and bare feet with the push broom, Buster close behind, yipping and growling. "Drop the coat, boy!"

I unzipped and dropped my coat, turning to face the snarling, furry menace attacking it. Grandpa Liam shouted again, "Grab the ax. Hit him with the blunt end!"

"Shouldn't I get the .22?"

"No! You'll be more likely to shoot one of us or Buster. He's too fast to get a decent shot anyways."

The fisher lunged at Grandpa Liam now, snapping the broom handle in his teeth. I had no idea something that size could be so powerful. The ax was next to the cabin door, so I seized it and clenched it in both hands, looking for an opportunity.

The fisher seemed focused on Grandpa Liam now and Buster by his side. I swung once, furtively, out of fear that I might hit Buster. Then I slowed down and watched the pattern of his attack—feint, hiss, lunge, retreat, repeat. I hoisted the ax above my head and swung hard on his retreat, catching him right on the back of the head. The fisher dropped in the snow.

"Stand on his chest, Ez." Grandpa Liam was breathing hard now but smiling wide. "Make sure he's not just stunned. Stand on his chest for three whole minutes."

I did what I was told. When it was over, Grandpa Liam walked up and gave me a hard clap on the shoulder. "There are easier ways to catch a fisher, but I'm glad you're on my side."

I smiled and breathed a sigh of relief. "Why did you tell me to hit him with the blunt end?"

"An adult fisher is worth $120. There was no need to ruin the hide."

I'm sure the look on my face was completely incredulous.

"What? I knew you'd get him." We stood there looking at each other for a moment—Grandpa Liam amused, and me still in shock.

"Look," Grandpa Liam said, motioning back to the shed. There was another fisher already dead in my trap. He turned and strode through the snow, back into the cabin, still in long johns and bare feet, but hollering over his shoulder, "We're off to a great start today."

Chapter 25

THE CHANGES IN THE woods were accelerating every day. On colder nights, we could hear the lake ice crack and whine in eerie, ominous soundwaves. Grandpa Liam was trying to teach me every last detail he could. One day we stood at the shore of Manidookaan in our bibs and trapping coats, eyeing Chief's Ridge on the far side of the lake, listening to the ice whine and rumble for a long time.

"The big lakes sound scary when they make noises like that, but that's actually from the ice expanding when it's cold, not from it contracting or weakening. Sometimes you'll get huge ice ridges in the spring. If you drive across the ice this time of the year, you have to go slower. Hitting an ice ridge is like driving headlong into a brick wall."

"I guess Nora's dad died by going through the ice."

"It was horrible, Ezra. Ruth was so devastated. She never married again, and she was still a young woman. I think she just took all the love she had for her husband and gave it to Nora after that."

"I can see that." I waited for a minute, then added, "Grandpa, can I ask you another question?" The question had been gnawing at me since I saw him looking at the pictures from his box, but it never felt like the right time to ask until now.

He turned to look at me and raised one white, wispy eyebrow.

"How come you never had more kids other than my dad? You're such a good dad, and you love kids and Grandma Emma so much. An old alpha like you should lead the biggest pack on the rez."

My question struck an unexpected nerve. Grandpa Liam coughed and turned away. I thought he might even be on the verge of tears. I was taken aback.

"Grandpa Liam? I'm sorry. You don't have to answer that."

There was a long, grave pause, and then Grandpa Liam turned back to me and coughed again. "No, Ezra. I do."

Whatever was coming next felt like it might be heavier than I could lift. I fought the urge to turn away too and looked into his handsomely wrinkled face. His normally mirth-filled eyes were troubled.

"Ezra, I need to tell you the story of Ethan and Olivia. I have carried this story in the center of my heart and the front of my mind for over forty years, but I have never given it voice. Grandma Emma and Byron know this story. They've lived it with me. But I even forbade them from sharing it. I'm not a controlling man, but the pain was too much for me to bear. I'm not proud of myself, but I denied my pain and theirs. It's like this feeling was frozen in me. But it needs to melt. It needs to come out."

"You really don't have to, Grandpa."

"It's taken me this long to get wise. I can't back down now. You'll see all of us a little differently after you hear this, Ezra. But I promise, it really will be okay. I want you to find your heart and give it voice, so I must do the same."

We both took a deep breath, then he began.

"I love your Grandma Emma with a fire that will burn through the ages. I always have. We grew up together, but I was seventeen years old when I knew that I wanted to date her and she was sixteen. Our parents forbade us to marry until we were both eighteen. We married on Emma's eighteenth birthday. My greatest ambition was to make her happy and have as many children as the Creator and all the spirits of the land would give us."

I kept watching Grandpa Liam's face. This was exactly how I imagined their relationship getting started.

Grandpa Liam continued: "We waited a little while to have children so I could save up enough money to get us a proper house and have everything we needed for our family."

"I always wondered how you paid for everything."

"It took some effort because trapping requires such a big investment in traps and equipment. Then we had a beautiful baby boy and named him Ethan. He was hilarious, even as a baby. He had a big, round face like your Grandma Emma, and he had a laugh like me. He loved to laugh. And two years later we had a daughter, Olivia. She was a little shy compared to Ethan, but bright and inquisitive: she filled our home with happiness. Only a year after that, we had Byron. My pack was off to a pretty good start."

I could easily picture a young Grandpa Liam sitting in a big chair and reading books or telling stories to his children. He was a natural.

"Emma had a little trouble with Byron's birth, so we decided to wait a couple years before trying for a fourth child. Then, disaster struck."

I swallowed, unsure of what was coming next.

"The Canadian Department of Indian Affairs had been busy swooping up Native kids and sending them to residential boarding schools since the 1800s. Over one third of our people went to these schools. Most people know that these schools beat the children for speaking our language, and mistreated them in all kinds of ways, using them for manual labor and depriving them of any kind of nurture or even proper nutrition. What a lot of people don't know is how many children died at the schools."

Grandpa Liam's voice strained and cracked, but he seemed determined to finish his story. I wasn't sure if I should look away while he spoke or give him a hug. I just stood there and listened.

"The DIA couldn't handle the volume of Native kids they were taking from their parents, so they paid churches to run many of the schools. The Brandon Indian Residential School in Brandon, Manitoba, took Ethan and Olivia. That school was started by the Methodists, but the Catholics took over by the time our sweet babies went there."

"There was no way to stop them?"

"There was no way. It happened to everyone. If you hid, they found you. Then your kids went to the schools, and you went to jail. There was nothing we could do."

I suddenly felt like punching something again. I took a deep breath.

"We were good parents. We provided for their every need. We loved them so much. All they knew was love and nurture and laughter. Emma cried every day when they were taken from us. The school separated the children by age and gender, so Ethan and Olivia didn't even get to see each other. They must have been so scared."

"Grandpa, I'm so sorry."

He touched my shoulder for a second. "There's more."

"I want to know. What happened to them?"

"We got some information out of the Truth and Reconciliation Commission some years ago. There was a picture of Ethan, with his hair cut off, wearing a uniform. His big, round face was unmistakable. The kids were in some of the school attendance records."

These must have been the pictures and papers in his box.

"Olivia got tuberculosis. They buried her at the school. Once she left for school, we never saw her again. They didn't even send her body back or give us any choice in the kind of sendoff she would get. The Catholics probably called her case a successful conversion—a win for the church. But we know what really happened. They deprived her of her human rights and murdered her. We got a letter saying that she died six months after her burial."

I felt a lurching sensation in my stomach. "This makes me so sad."

"Me too." Grandpa Liam sighed.

I noticed that my hands were bunched into fists. "And mad."

"Me too, my boy. Me too. We had no contact with the kids, even though we tried everything. Ethan lived for two more years, as far as we can tell. The school records showed that he was being disciplined more and more. Eventually, it was daily. All he did was laugh when he was with us. He wasn't a problem child. The school didn't even send us a letter on him. When the TRC took testimony and did investigations, they told us that they think he died from physical abuse or trauma given the records they found. He was probably one of the kids in the mass graves they discovered there years later."

I felt a lump in my throat just listening to the pain in my grandpa's voice. I could hardly imagine what it must have been like to live through that.

"My children were just statistics to the churches and the Canadian government—two of the many thousands who died at the schools. They weren't even worth making marked graves to the school officials. But they were everything to us."

I touched Grandpa Liam's shoulder, but just for a moment.

"I did everything I could to save my babies, Ezra. But it wasn't enough. Emma and I couldn't bring more children into the world after that. And we vowed that they would never get their hands on Byron. We took everything we owned and went into the wilderness. We built the trapping cabin, and we raised Byron here. We put our roots here, in this sacred place, where the worlds meet, so we could be close to our babies dancing in the sky and keep close our sole remaining child dancing on this earth."

There were tears welling in Grandpa Liam's eyes now. Not knowing what to do, I instinctively reached out and placed my hand on his shoulder, but this time I kept it there. He turned and patted me on the cheek, then pulled me into a tight embrace and wept.

It took a while for Grandpa Liam to regain his composure. I had never seen a grown man cry like that before. "Miigwech, my boy. Don't be alarmed. It's good for us to cry once in a while. I was holding that one in for far too long."

We both pulled in a long, heavy breath and let it go.

Chapter 26

GRANDPA LIAM and I pulled all the traps and snares for good the third week of March. It took us two whole days to break down the line, clean all the animals, and square away the cabin. The snowmobile sled was fully loaded and secured with ratchet straps by the end of the second day. It was our final night in the cabin for the season.

The ice would soften in April and break up in May. We were planning to spend most of the summer at the rez or fishing on Ottertail Lake or Rainy Lake nearby, where the walleyes and smallmouth bass reigned. I did a little homework and Grandpa Liam read. He called me over to the rocking chair after that and showed me some of the contents of his secret wooden box. There was an article in there about Grandpa Liam winning a beaver skinning contest at seventeen years of age and a picture of Ethan, Olivia, and Byron. He seemed less closed and wounded now—buoyant even—and happy to share about them.

I woke in the morning to the strange sound of Buster growling. I had never heard him growl like that before. But he was going out of his mind. His head was low to the floor and he was staring at the cabin door with a low, steady growl rumbling in his throat. I looked around to get my bearings. There was already sunlight streaming through the east window of the cabin and steaming oatmeal on the table. Grandpa Liam was standing behind the kitchen table in Dickies and suspenders, thumbing shells into the clip of the 7mm Remington Magnum.

"What's going on?"

"We've got unexpected company."

I saw a shadow pass by the east window. There was definitely something out there. "What is it, Grandpa?"

"We're in a heap of trouble, Ezra. That's not a regular animal out there. That's Chi."

"Chi? The bear?!"

"He must have woken up a little early this year. And he probably hasn't eaten since he started his hibernation."

"Is he hoping to eat us?"

"No. Bears don't usually prey on people. He's probably just hoping to get his paws on our food."

"Then let's just leave the food and take the hides and get out of here!" I exclaimed.

"That's the plan. But the scent of our food and hides is on everything, even our clothes. He'd be happy to see for himself if there's anything good to eat. So we can't give him a chance. He's probably just scavenging. But bears can be territorial and sometimes perceive humans as a threat. Bears are unpredictable. There is often a reason when a bear mauls a human, but they don't need a reason to attack."

"Tell me what to do."

"Ezra, we are going to stay in the cabin until he wanders off and then we'll get on the Ski-Doo and waste no time getting back to the rez. One of us can drive and the other can keep the 7mm ready."

I peeked out the east window and caught a big, slow, brown movement next to the wood rick. It must have been Chi, but the bolts of wood were still stacked high and obscured a certain view.

"I think he's still there. Should I get the .22 so we have two rifles?"

Grandpa Liam was pacing the cabin, clearly anxious.

"No. The caliber is so small on that, it'll just make him mad. The 7mm has enough knock-down power to handle a bear. But the best way to handle this is just not be here when he's around. The rifle is just a precaution. We won't be looking for trouble. I can't risk you, Ezra. Your dad would never forgive me if something happened to you. I'd never forgive myself."

"You're scaring me, Grandpa."

"We have reason to be scared." His eyes moved quickly, scanning the room. I had never seen him agitated like this. He pointed to the satellite phone my dad sent with us when we opened the trapline. "Help me figure that thing out."

I grabbed the satellite phone. Grandpa Liam moved from window to window, looking for signs of the bear. After a few moments, he said, "I think he left, Ezra. Let's give it a little more time to be sure."

The satellite phone was an Iridium Extreme. It probably cost my dad $2,000 between it and the prepaid usage. The controls were intuitive, even though it took a few minutes to establish a link.

"I think it's working."

"Call your dad first."

I punched in the number for my dad's smartphone and hit send. He picked up right away.

"Dad, it's me."

"Ezra, is everything okay?" His voiced sounded stressed. I'm sure he wasn't expecting a call from the satellite phone.

"Yeah, we are fine. Grandpa wanted me to call you. We're coming back to the rez."

My dad breathed a sigh of relief. "Thanks for letting me know. I'm in Northeast now, but I'm planning to come up north tomorrow. That's unlike your grandpa to lower himself to using the satellite phone, though. What's going on?"

"Chi woke up. He's been sniffing around the cabin."

The tension was instantly back. I could hear the chair he was sitting in creak and then roll. He must have stood straight up. "Ezra, you can't take any chances with that animal. Get on the Ski-Doo and come right back. You can't outrun a bear on your feet. But you can outrun him on a snowmobile. I'm going to cancel my classes today and come up north now. Keep the 7mm in one hand and the satellite phone in the other until you're back."

I pulled on my bibs and donned my trapping jacket in record time. Grandpa handed me the 7mm. "I'll drive. You'll hold this. Buster can ride with me so there's nothing in the way if you need to shoot."

We waited for an hour to make double sure Chi wasn't lurking around the cabin, cautiously eyeing the door and listening for any sign of movement outside. Then we grabbed any remaining gear still in the cabin for the trip back to the rez. Buster was back to his normal state of excitement. Grandpa Liam seemed reassured by that.

We opened the cabin door to a winterscape bathed in sunlight. Grandpa put his sunglasses on. There were bear tracks all over the cabin yard—huge paw prints deep in the melting snow. Chi seemed to have been more interested in the shed than the hides and beaver meat in the Ski-Doo's game sled.

"Grandpa, why didn't he just tear apart the game sled?"

"The fisher hides. Their scent glands are bear repellent. Fishers will spray their food when they cache it. No wolf or bear will touch it after that. We just lucked out that the fisher hides were on top of the pile and that they were enough. I bet Chi is still pretty hungry."

We hurriedly mounted the Ski-Doo and took off. We were fully loaded, and the March snowstorms over the past few weeks made the trail back to Rainy Lake slow going. We were only several hundred yards from the cabin when Grandpa stopped.

His body was tense, and his eyes scanned the tree line nervously. He hopped off the Ski-Doo. "Deadfall. I'll have to get the chainsaw. You just keep your eyes open."

Buster was smart enough to sit on the Ski-Doo and avoid the deep snow. Grandpa Liam focused on getting the chainsaw out of the game sled and re-cinching the ratchets, so he could keep it handy in case we ran into any other down trees. He was just getting ready to start the saw up when Buster started growling again. At first, it seemed like he was growling at me, but I knew better than that and slowly turned my head to see Chi standing just twenty yards behind me. The sheer enormity of the animal made me tremble.

"Don't move, Ezra," Grandpa Liam whispered from my side. "If he charges, he'll be on you before you can get around to shoot."

"What should I do?" I hissed.

"I will try to distract him by starting the chainsaw. Maybe the sound will scare him away. If he runs away, we cut this log, get on the Ski-Doo, and get out of here. If he charges me, turn and shoot him."

Chi's head was rocking side to side through our conversation, as if he was following our voices back and forth. Grandpa Liam lifted the chainsaw, depressed the gas trigger, and flipped the choke. Then he pulled the starter cord. The saw sputtered, but didn't start, and in an astonishing burst of furious speed, Chi charged.

I turned as fast as I could, raising the 7mm and flipping off the safety. Grandpa Liam yelled at the top of his voice and raised the chainsaw in front of him. Chi whirled at the sound, and now Grandpa Liam was right between me and Chi. There was no way to shoot.

"Shoot that thing in the air, boy!"

I raised the 7mm and fired off a round in the air. The sharp report startled Chi and he stood on all four legs, bristling, just yards from Grandpa Liam. Buster's fervid barking provided little distraction.

I shot in the air again and Chi gave a low *whoof*. But his gaze remained fixed on Grandpa Liam, and the beast didn't move.

"Ezra, there's a jack pine right behind you. Chi is too big to climb trees the way smaller bears do. Slowly walk backward to that tree. Keep the rifle ready in case you get a shot. If you do, take it. If not, climb up fifteen feet, out of this thing's reach. That should give you a safe angle to shoot him no matter where I am or what's happening."

I had never been so scared in my life. I started to move backwards to the tree, slow enough so I wouldn't trip on something under the snow. I kept the rifle raised and ready. Chi and Grandpa Liam had their eyes locked on each other, the bear rocking back and forth in his stance, and Grandpa Liam fixed and unflinching.

I made it to the base of the jack pine and pointed the rifle up, shooting it in the air a third time. Buster jumped off the snowmobile, floundering in the deep powder and making his way next to Grandpa Liam, barking frantically.

"Ezra, don't shoot again unless you have a safe shot! The 7mm only holds three shots in the clip and one in the magazine. We need to make that last shot count. Start climbing."

Chi was still rocking back forth on all fours, eyes on Grandpa Liam. As fast as I could, I slung the rifle over my shoulder, reached the nearest branch, and started to climb. No lynx climbed a tree as fast as I climbed that day. As soon as I was high enough to get a shot, I turned to get the scope locked on the bear, but I realized Chi had shifted his attention to me now. And just as I had gotten settled, he burst past Grandpa Liam and charged the jack pine where I was perched. The power of his body striking the tree knocked accumulated snow from the branches, showering it down in all directions. My body shook with such force that I had to grab the nearest branch with my left arm. I watched in horror as the 7mm Remington Magnum slipped from my right, tumbling through the branches to the snow-covered ground below.

Chi stood on his hind legs and pushed on the tree with all his might. I held on to the trunk with all my strength. My thoughts darted, fast and feverish: I was the last of my grandfather's line. I had to live—to live for Ethan and Olivia, my dad, my grandparents, and all those who came before us.

The tree was swaying wildly now, and I was barely hanging on. Then, behind Chi, I saw a flash of brown and gray. Grandpa Liam was running straight at the bear, a long knife in his hand. He collided with the creature, screaming and stabbing with unrestrained fury.

Chi spun around and issued a tremendous roar, knocking Grandpa Liam to the ground and descending on him with outstretched paws. There was nothing I could do but watch and listen to the sickening crunch of claws on bone.

Buster was still barking and jumping to no effect. Chi pawed and bit at Grandpa Liam's now prostrate body. I could see blood in the snow.

Then came another flash of brown and gray. And another. And another. A lush and savage growl filled the woods with terrifying intensity, quickly joined in an ensemble of primal power.

Ogimaa lunged first, latching on to Chi's fur and flesh. His teeth stayed clenched tighter than a Conibear trap as he sprang back, ripping a massive, gaping red horror from Chi's neck. Ogimaa continued to pull, tearing Chi's hide past his shoulder, effectively starting to skin him alive. Chi gave a ferocious roar and whirled in defense, but Ogimaa released him and darted out of the way. Two more wolves charged Chi's opposite flank. When he turned to claw them, Ogimaa attacked again from the other side. The entire pack followed in organized precision until every limb of the massive beast had yawning wounds and wolves of every color were tearing, holding, and immobilizing their enemy.

Chi was enormous, ferocious, and powerful. But he was no match for the pack. The struggle raged for several minutes more, but Chi eventually collapsed just thirty yards from where the wolves first attacked him. Time stood still for one ravenous heartbeat while they gorged on his flesh. Then in streaks of black, brown, and gray they were gone, leaving nothing but the blood-stained snow and me, climbing down from the jack pine to the supine form of my beloved Grandpa Liam, my heart sinking in my chest.

Fort Frances

Chapter 27

I STUDIED Grandpa Liam's face from where I stood. I wasn't ready to get any closer. His weathered brown skin and handsome wrinkles were framed in a halo of thin, white hair. There wasn't even any blood on his face. But he wasn't moving. And his jacket and bibs were raked with claw marks and covered in blood.

"Grandpa Liam?" My voice trembled with heartache.

Everything had happened so fast that I'd lost track of Buster, who emerged from a hiding place under the balsams nearby and joined me. He started licking Grandpa Liam's cheek. I wanted to cough or throw up, but nothing would come out. I looked away.

"For such a small animal, he sure has some big odor. We should get him a doggy toothbrush. Ugh."

The sound of the familiar voice jolted me out of my head. "Grandpa?!"

"Always."

He was alive. "Grandpa!" I rushed to his side.

"Ezra, are you hurt?"

"Am I hurt? No. Are you kidding? I thought you were dead."

"Me too. I still might die, Ezra. This feels worse than it looks."

"What should I do?"

"You're going to have to try to stop the bleeding first. Then call 911."

I unzipped my coat and pulled off my shirt, tearing it into long strips. I sat him up and pulled his coat off. There was blood everywhere from gaping lacerations across his ribs and abdomen. There was a massive bite mark on his left forearm and the bones there were broken and displaced. He must have been trying to fight off the attack with his hands when he got that one. I wrapped and tied his abdomen and chest as best I could and helped him to the Ski-Doo so he could sit.

I called 911 on the satellite phone. It only took a minute to get through, but it felt like an eternity. My gaze surveyed the scene around us. There were wolf tracks everywhere and a massive bloody stain in the snow where Chi was killed. The wolves hadn't left much behind but the blood, tracks, and few scattered bear bones. It didn't even seem real.

A crisp woman's voice snapped from the satellite phone. "What's the nature of your emergency?"

"We need your help. We've been attacked by a bear. My Grandpa Liam is hurt bad."

"Okay, we will dispatch help as soon as we can. Where are you located?"

"We're on a trapline north of Red Gut Bay."

"Are you calling from a satellite phone?"

"Yes." My voice must have sounded panicky.

"Stay calm, sir. What model of satellite phone do you have?"

"It's an Iridium Extreme."

"Okay. Look at the face of the phone. Do you see a yellow button with an arrow on it?"

"Yes."

"Press and hold that for five seconds, okay?"

"Okay." I held the button.

"Give me just a second."

"Please hurry."

She came back just a minute later. "Leave the phone on. We have your location by GPS and we can track you as long as the phone is on."

"Okay."

"Listen now. There is no way for us get a helicopter to land near you because it is so densely wooded. We can get a helicopter to the lake nearby and then have a rescue team hike in, unless you have a way to get your grandpa to the lake."

"I can get him to the ice road on Rainy Lake toward Bear Pass. It's not far. We have a snow machine here."

"Okay. Navigate to the ice road and leave the phone on so we can track you."

I went into action after that. I had to cut the log across the trail. Grandpa Liam was weak, but he still made me retrieve the rifle, the chainsaw, his knife, and his hat. I had to put his bloody coat back on him and seat him in front of me with my hands on the throttle and handles in case he passed out during the trip.

As soon as I got us in the open on the ice road, we stopped. More jostling on the snowmobile would just make him bleed more. The helicopter rescue team found us as soon as we made it to the lake. Within five minutes, they had him loaded on a gurney and lifting off from the ice. I sat on the Skandic and clutched Buster close for one long, heartrending minute.

I called my dad then on the satellite phone. He picked up right away. "Ezra?"

"Yeah, it's me."

"Are you okay?" His voice was strained.

My voice sounded hoarse as I stammered a response: "No. I mean . . . I'm okay. I'm not hurt. But Grandpa Liam . . . Chi got him. He's alive, but he's hurt really bad."

"Where are you?"

I couldn't think of how to respond. I felt like a white pine covered in hoarfrost, immobilized by cold.

"Ezra?"

"Sorry . . . I . . . I'm on the ice road from the bay to Bear Pass. I already called 911. Grandpa Liam is in a helicopter on his way to Fort Frances."

"Oh my God. Ezra, I am so glad that you're not hurt. I am going to call Grandma Emma. I'll have her meet you at Bear Pass and give you a ride to the hospital. Start the ride to Bear Pass now. She'll be waiting when you get there. I'll meet you in Fort Frances as soon as I can."

"Okay."

I swooped up Buster, hopped on the Skandic, and sped to Bear Pass as fast as I could. Grandma Emma was waiting at the landing there with Grandpa Liam's truck and trailer when I arrived. I jumped off the snow machine and ran up to her. She looked like a loon whose nest had just been raided by mink, ready to spill a mournful cry into the wilderness. I just hugged her and held on. Neither one of us could bring ourselves to say anything.

We loaded the Ski-Doo and sled in strained silence and went straight to the hospital at Fort Frances. My dad was on his way from Minneapolis, but it would be a few more hours before he arrived.

We made it to the La Verendrye Hospital in Fort Frances in forty-five minutes. We left Buster in the truck and rushed inside, hoping to see Grandpa Liam right away, but he was in surgery. We spent three hours in the waiting room. I started missing my smartphone, back on the rez in Grandpa and Grandma's house. Grandma Emma kept leaving the waiting room to ask the nurses for updates, but I think they started to get annoyed with her. Every time the door to the waiting room opened, our heads snapped up to see if it was the doctor with an update.

The bear, the wolves, and the rescue still had me surging with stress and adrenaline. The waiting room of the La Verendrye Hospital in Fort Frances now had all of us grinding in a different kind of stress.

The door burst open after a few hours of waiting and my dad strode across the room in two quick steps. Grandma Emma and I rose to our feet and he crushed us both in a tight hug.

"Any news from the doctor?" he asked.

"Not yet," Grandma Emma answered. The disappointment in her voice was obvious.

We all went to sit, but the door opened again before we could. This time, it was the surgeon, Dr. Arnaud. He was a small man with more hair on his forearms than the top of his head. He still had blue scrubs on when he came in, peering at us through thick gold-framed eyeglasses.

"Thank you for your patience. Are you all Liam Cloud's family?"

"Yes," Grandma Emma replied.

"Very well. I'm here to give you an update on Liam."

We all held our breath.

"He's alive, but gravely injured. We had to operate right away because he had a lot of internal bleeding. Usually, cases like this get sent to Thunder Bay because they have a bigger surgery ward with more specialists."

My dad and Grandma Emma gave each other a meaningful look.

Dr. Arnaud continued, "Liam has multiple displaced fractures in both of his left forearm bones from a bear bite. We had to set the bones with pins. He has two big rows of stitches on the arm, one from the surgery and the other from the bear bite. I feel confident about that part of the surgery."

"What about his internal bleeding?" Grandma Emma interjected, her words fast and anxious.

"I was getting to that. We had to do another surgery on his abdomen because the bear raked his chest and belly. We've stopped the bleeding. He does have some broken ribs. That is probably what will hurt the most. But the greatest danger is not actually the injuries themselves. The danger is infection. We cleaned everything as carefully and methodically as possible, but bear bites carry bacteria. Even the smallest amount can cause a lot of trouble. We won't have an answer for you on that for a couple of days."

"Can we see him?"

"Yes, of course. He's sedated and likely to sleep for a couple more hours. But you can see him any time now. He's in the ICU, room number 4."

"Thank you," Grandma Emma replied.

"I'll show you the way."

My dad, Grandma, and I followed Dr. Arnaud down the corridor to a secure wing of the hospital, then up an elevator to the ICU. La Verendrye was a fraction of the size of Hennepin County Medical Center, but the vibe was much the same: sterile, white lights, and muted stress in nearly everyone we saw. Dr. Arnaud pointed to room 4 and turned away to the nurse's station.

Grandpa Liam looked healthy and peaceful in his hospital bed. His skin was brown and vibrant, even in the fluorescent light. His arm was bandaged from wrist to armpit and his chest was bandaged from his armpits to his groin. He was the toughest seventy-four-year-old man I'd ever met. If anyone could charge a giant bear with a knife and live to tell the tale, it was my Grandpa Liam.

Grandma Emma sat by the bed and held his hand. My dad stood behind her. I circled around to the other side of the bed and kissed him on the forehead.

"There's probably an easier way to impress your girl, Grandpa. I recommend one of the easier ways."

Grandma Emma smiled at that, but there were tears in her eyes.

My dad texted Stanley to come get Buster from the truck and bring him to the rez. My dad and I slept in the hospital waiting room the first night. Grandma Emma slept in the recliner in Grandpa Liam's room.

AT THE END OF the second day in the hospital, Dr. Arnaud said that Grandpa Liam did have a staph infection. It was likely to be a long fight. Grandma Emma refused to leave his side, so my dad drove me back to the rez in Grandpa Liam's truck so we could unload the Ski-Doo and hides, shower and sleep, check on Buster, and grab supplies to run back to Grandma Emma.

I powered on my smart phone as soon as we arrived at Grandpa and Grandma's house. I texted updates to

Nora, Noah, Oliver, Amelia, and my cousin Elroy. I even texted Daniel Drumbeater. He was a pipe carrier. Maybe he could pray for Grandpa Liam.

Nora texted back right away: *OMG, Ezra. I am so sorry to hear about Grandpa Liam.*

I don't know if he's gonna make it.

I'm here for you either way.

I know. That means a lot.

I set up my bedroll on the couch and then she texted again.

Do you want an update on Northeast?

Sure.

No news is good news. Nothing new in the investigation. And still no sign of Matt.

That's good. I've had enough drama this week.

No doubt.

Have a good night, Nora.

I'd give you a big kiss if I was at Red Gut right now.

It's the thought that counts.

The thought counts, but the real thing is even better.

I have to agree with you on that. I'll text again tomorrow.

Chapter 28

ON GRANDPA LIAM'S THIRD evening in the hospital, my dad finally convinced Grandma Emma to let him feed her a proper meal at the hospital cafeteria. I stayed with Grandpa Liam under strict instructions to call them if anything changed with his condition. He seemed dramatically worse than his first day in the hospital. His skin looked like it had a thin layer of watery ash rubbed all over it. It was gray and clammy in appearance. He was running an obvious fever. He wasn't sedated, though he did have morphine drip. He slept a lot.

It was strange to see him in a hospital gown. They should have at least let him wear suspenders. The gown and his condition left him looking weak and emasculated.

I was wearing blue jeans and a tee shirt. I went to the little particle board armoire and fished out Grandpa Liam's green Fort Frances Fur Trapping Days tee shirt and red suspenders. Grandma Emma had us bring fresh clothes for him, hoping for a return home soon. I took off my shirt and put his on, which was a little tight, but not so tight that I would do it damage. It still smelled like Grandpa Liam. I latched his suspenders on to my jeans too and sat in the reclining chair next to his bed. I texted Nora for a couple minutes while he slept and then scrolled TikTok.

I got up a little later and turned the fluorescent lights off, just using the tiny lamp by the nurse station to keep an eye on Grandpa Liam. He was still fast asleep. I put my phone down and closed my eyes for just a second. I didn't mean to fall asleep, but the dream pulled me in right away.

I was back at Chief's Ridge, near my rabbit snares, where I had first seen Ogimaa. The wolves were there all around me, circling me over and over and then bolting for the lake at Manidookaan. They wanted me to follow.

My nostrils flared in the cold wind, filled with the scent of balsam boughs, piney and pleasant. I ran after them, as fast as the pack. I could smell the faint odor of snowshoe hares as we crossed the rabbit trails. I wanted to turn and follow the scent, but Ogimaa urged the pack forward. Again, I followed, panting from the exertion.

I could taste things too: snowflakes hitting my lips, and blood from the back of my throat. Bear blood, like I had eaten from their kill. I let my tongue hang out of my mouth in spite of the cold and savored it all. I wanted to howl.

Within minutes we came to the shore of Manidoo-kaan and raced onto the ice. Only then did I notice the woman running with us. She was petite and brown, wearing jeans and a jean jacket and weathered Chuck Taylor shoes, totally out of place in the deep cold. I recognized her.

I stopped running, my mouth still open, and stood on the ice. Ogimaa turned and the wolves ringed us, trotting in circles.

"Mom?" I could see her face, the light lines by her eyes—bright and full of life—and her smile. Suddenly, all the memories I had begun fervently pouring into my notebook had all their missing details.

It felt like the wind was making my eyes water, but I dared not wipe them for fear of breaking my gaze. Whether it was the exertion of my run or the frigid air filling my lungs, I felt momentary panic trying to inhale. I wheezed in and strained my voice one more time, "Mom?"

She stood next to me, her chest rising and falling, catching her breath. "My sweet son. What a beautiful man you have become. I have missed you so much."

"Are you real?"

"I am real. I always was. I always will be. I just changed worlds."

My mind flashed to Grandpa Liam telling me about changing worlds on the shore of Manidookaan. It suddenly seemed so long ago now. I looked at her and sighed. "Are you here for me?"

"No, my boy. It's good to see you, but I came for Grandpa Liam."

The wolves started to howl then, smothering any further words in yips and wails. I closed my eyes and yelled for them to stop, but my voice caught deep in my throat and I started to cough, coughing until my eyes popped open.

Grandpa Liam was looking at me back in the hospital room. I was out of breath.

"I had a dream," I said simply.

"I could tell," he whispered. He studied me for a long moment. I wished he didn't look so weak.

"I'll have the nurse get you a food tray."

He grimaced as he tried to sit up, then relaxed back into the pillow. "Is there a way to get Hulu in here?"

I texted my dad: *Grandpa's awake.*

When my dad and Grandma Emma returned, I got Hulu loaded on my dad's laptop so we could watch *Reservation Dogs*. It was different watching television without Buster and with Grandpa Liam giving muted chuckles, rather than his usual bellowing laugh. But it was still sweet to be together.

We watched one episode and then my dad and I went back to the rez to sleep. Rita came to the hospital to sit with Grandma Emma. She had come a couple of times before, but she'd started staying longer now, especially in the hours when Emma was the only family there with Liam.

The next morning, my dad dropped me off at the hospital again and went after groceries for the house. I went to Grandpa Liam's room, but I waited outside the door for a minute in case they were giving him a sponge bath or changing his bandages. I peeked through the door and saw just Grandpa Liam and Grandma Emma looking at each other. They weren't even talking. I thought about going in, but it seemed like I might be intruding.

Grandpa Liam finally spoke, his voice warm but tired: "I waited all these years to bring that boy trapping. I wanted to give him a chance to fall in love with the wilderness the way I did. You know the most amazing thing, Emma? I think it worked. He's not a boy anymore. He's a man. A true man of the woods. It's in his bones. Even the wolves know him. And he knows them. It's the second greatest success of my life. I'm truly proud of him."

I could see Grandma Emma holding his hand through the crack in the door.

"Do you want to know the craziest thing about our time on the trapline? I brought him there to help Byron save him—to help save him from Northeast Minneapolis, to help save him from himself. But I was the one who needed healing. I held on to my pain from losing Ethan and Olivia for too long. When I finally gave it voice, it went with the wind. I feel so much lighter. I just wish I found the courage to do it earlier." His voice sounded faint and strained. "I'm sorry I burdened you by making it unspeakable. You needed to heal too. We should have just faced it together."

"We did in our own way, my love." Her voice trembled slightly.

"That's the irony, Emma. I brought Ezra there to save him, but he was the one who saved me."

She pulled her hand from his and touched his face.

Grandpa Liam continued, "Do you want to know the greatest success of my life?"

"Tell me, Liam."

"It was skinning, stretching, and scraping that jumbo brown beaver in seventeen minutes flat at the Fort

Frances Fur Trapping Days when I was seventeen years old."

She gave a little snort and smiled at him. "You've always been impressive with a skinning knife, my love."

"I won a trophy for that, and a hundred dollars."

"I remember."

"Of course you do. You were the one handing out the trophies for the festivity board. When our hands touched, you cast a spell on me."

Emma laughed and slapped his hand ever so gently.

"You see, my dear, sweet Emma, the greatest success of my life was you. I am so grateful for us."

"Me too, Liam. Me too." Then she grabbed his good hand in both of hers.

"I really wanted to finish *Reservation Dogs*. But I don't know if I'm going to make it. I guess we all go in the middle of something."

She was squeezing his hand now. "You're going to make it."

"Well, if I don't, you'll have to finish the series and tell me what happened when you come to find me in the spirit world. Just take your time coming to join me. There's so much to live for."

I could tell that Grandma Emma was getting emotional, on the verge of weeping. I wasn't sure if I should stay or go.

Grandpa Liam interrupted her before she could get too sad.

"Promise me something."

"Anything."

"Promise me you'll tell the people that I died making love to you in the hospital bed, instead of from a staph infection."

Grandma Emma started laughing again, even pulling one hand back to her mouth and rocking back and forth.

Grandpa Liam laughed too and held on to her other hand. "I'll be the most famous Native man ever. A true hero to everyone at Red Gut. They'll be talking about it for generations."

Emma's giggles calmed into smiling eyes and then a frown crossed her brow. "I love you, Liam."

"I love you too." He paused for a second and then said, "One last thing, Emma. And I have to whisper this one so your grandson doesn't hear us outside the door."

What? How did he know I was there?

Grandma Emma leaned in, and that last secret was theirs alone.

Grandpa Liam's voice seemed a little faint as he called my name. I came to his side as quickly as I could. His skin looked even grayer and somehow thinner than I remembered. His hair was damp with sweat and matted to his forehead. I sat on the edge of his bed and leaned in so he wouldn't have to strain his voice.

"I have a couple jobs for you, Ezra."

"Whatever you need."

"First, I have some papers here. When you go back to the rez, put these in the kitchen somewhere obvious and easy to find."

"Sure."

"Second, when you go back to the rez, bring Buster to the hospital and sneak him in here with you. You might have to dodge the nurses. It'll probably do that mutt some good. He has the body of a large gerbil but the heart of a timber wolf. We're his pack and he needs us."

"I'm on it." It felt good to know there was something meaningful I could actually do. I'd felt so helpless sitting in the hospital day after day. Now I had a chore list, and I was ready to spring into eager action. I started to rise, but Grandpa Liam tapped my forearm. I was so used to him giving me a gruff slap on the shoulder that his gentle tap seemed unnerving. I sat back down.

"Lastly, let me give you some old-fashioned advice."

"Okay."

"All your dad wanted to do was love your mom the way I love my Emma, for the rest of his life. His big old heart is broken that it didn't work out that way. Mark Twain is full of crap, but one of the true things he wrote is that history doesn't repeat itself—but it echoes. Do you remember the story of Ethan and Olivia?"

"I'll never forget."

"When we lost them, we poured all our love into Byron. When Byron lost Isabelle, he poured everything into you. I know you've been mad at him. I know you've blamed him for not protecting your mom. But there was no way to know what would happen. And your mom didn't take orders from anyone, anyways. Her passing wasn't his fault. My advice is to quit turning away from him. Look him in the eyes. Tell him what you really feel. You've been the omega of this family long enough. It's time to join the pack."

His eyes were searching for mine. I noticed a slight reddish hue to his whites that hadn't been there before. I thought I could feel all the blood in my body rushing down to my feet, a quickening in my heartbeat, and a lump in my throat. My voice stammered. "I don't want you to die, Grandpa."

"Me either, Ezra. But we don't always get to choose. All trees must perish so the forest thrives." He winced a little, but he pulled his grimace into a smile and kept looking at me.

I moved from the bed to the recliner next to his bed. I knew he was fighting for his life. His voice was strained and raspy, but sweet. His eyelids seemed heavy and his blinking took longer than it should, but his gaze stayed focused on my face.

"Ezra, some people think growth only happens in the spring. Plants grow in the spring. People grow in the spring of their lives. But growth is more than a spring-time flood, it's a dance. Dance in all your seasons, my boy, and play the music loud."

Ottertail

Chapter 29

GRANDPA LIAM passed away while my dad and I were driving back to the rez to get Buster. Grandma Emma was the only one there, holding his hand. I think that's how he wanted it.

Losing him didn't hit me right away. I stayed busy helping my dad build Grandpa Liam's spirit fire in the yard back at Red Gut. We kept it going day and night. People came from all the families in the community to offer condolences and put tobacco in the fire. Daniel Drumbeater came every evening. Grandma Emma kept churning out food for the nonstop traffic. Rita Kingfisher came over to help. She was a good friend to Grandma Emma and often stayed later than necessary to visit and help clean my grandma's kitchen. It was a good thing that they had each other too. Natives loved to eat.

Two days later, Northridge Funeral Home brought Grandpa Liam's body to the community center. We used a metal bucket to get coals from the fire at the house and moved it over there. All the humans and food followed.

I put Grandpa Liam's papers in the kitchen like he'd asked. It didn't seem like anything important—cash receipts and a letter of some kind sealed in an envelope. I honored his wishes no matter how small.

Nora and Ruth came back to Rita's the day before the wake. She'd been asking me to take one of our walks down the housing road in our winter coats. The temperatures were just above freezing during the day now.

"Ezra, did your grandpa actually die, you know, being romantic with your grandma? My Grandma Rita was helping your grandma cook and that's the story she confided in her . . ."

I wanted to break into laughter. The thought of Grandma Emma spreading Grandpa Liam's fib around the rez seemed so ridiculous. But there was no way I was going interfere.

"Yeah. After his surgery, they chased all of us out of the hospital room so they could have alone time. Nobody thought that romance would be the end of him, but what a way to go!"

Nora laughed. I don't know if she or anyone else really believed it, but the rumor had a life of its own after that, and it seemed to make everything a little easier. People probably would share that story for generations.

We walked down to the landing. Daniel Drumbeater's ice house had been pulled off the lake to the shore with all the others. It seemed like ages ago when Nora and I saw the wolves chasing deer on the lake here, even though it was just a few months. As we turned back, my eyes followed the snowbank to Grandpa Liam and Grandma Emma's house. I half expected to see him standing in the yard, shoveling snow and making a funny face to embarrass me walking with Nora. I must have stopped walking and just stood, staring at the driveway.

"Ezra, did you know that eagles mate for life?"

My gaze shifted from the driveway to her face. I knew wolves did. I hadn't ever heard that about the eagles. "Really?"

"Yeah. Most birds do. But eagles have the most dramatic mating dance. They lock talons in mid-flight and plummet toward the earth, breaking apart right before they hit."

I glanced back at the driveway. "That's cool."

"Oh Ezra, I forgot to tell you! Mr. Lukas had a hickey on his neck at school."

My head whipped around. "What?"

"Yeah. I think he's dating the new English teacher, Ms. Erickson. At least someone at that school is having fun."

"That's hilarious. Did he seem embarrassed?"

"Actually, I think he was proud."

I laughed. We walked past my grandparents' house to Rita's. I came in for a visit while Nora baked chocolate chip cookies. They were warm and sweet.

THE MORNING OF GRANDPA Liam's wake, I jolted from my sleep to the sound of Buster growling. I had only heard him growl a couple times before, and it was a serious threat every time. My dad and Grandma Emma were both in the kitchen looking out the window.

"What's going on?"

"We have unexpected company, gwis." My dad's voice was tense.

I peered through the window next to my dad. Standing next to his imposing frame made me feel a little safer. There was a big white Chevy Suburban parked in the driveway, with police lights flashing on top and *Royal Canadian Mounted Police* stenciled on the side. Another RCMP cruiser was parked on the housing road, and a third car with no markings. We could see officers with the distinctive hats of RCMP patrol officers and a couple people wearing suits making their way to the house.

"Dad, why are they here?"

"I don't know, my boy."

"You boys don't do anything stupid," Grandma Emma said quietly, and she strode across the kitchen to the door and gently pulled it open.

Detective Williams was standing there with two RCMP officers.

"Good morning, Mrs. Cloud. Can we come in?"

"I thought you didn't have jurisdiction here, Mr. Williams." My dad's voice sounded curt and guarded.

"I don't have jurisdiction. But they do," he replied, motioning to the RCMP officers. "They are here to exercise a search warrant. We aren't taking interviews. We aren't taking anyone into custody. We're just exercising a search warrant on the property. I am here today as an observer, but we work together on a joint jurisdiction task force."

"Come in, please." Grandma Emma seemed far less concerned than she should have been. She turned and said, "Byron, why don't you take Ezra for a walk? This won't take long."

My dad seemed a little confused too, but he put his coat and boots on and motioned for me to do the same.

I felt like something wasn't right about all of this. We stepped outside and watched for a minute as several more officers entered the house. We started walking down the housing road toward the community center, but I stopped at the junction.

"Dad, can I go see Nora? I'll join you at the community center in a few minutes."

"Okay, gwis. Just don't go back to the house until the cops are done. Do you have any idea why they're there?"

"Not at all."

"Something's not right."

"I know."

I walked as fast as I could to Rita's and started pounding on the door. Nora answered quickly. The stress on my face must have been obvious. She donned her blue coat, boots, and Maple Leafs hat and mittens and came out for a walk and talk. I filled her in on the search warrant and ruminated on what it all could mean.

"Nora, it just doesn't make sense. How are the cops still not convinced?"

Nora gave me strange look, but her lips were pursed. We turned at the junction. I wasn't ready to be in mixed company at the community center and the cops were still at our house, so we walked up to the tribal government building where Daniel Drumbeater's office was located. It was a small building, just big enough for a meeting room and a few offices. It had a long porch next to the parking lot with an overhang, so it was free of snow. We sat on the edge of the porch, dangling our legs.

Nora drew a deep breath, staring at her boots, and then turned to face me. "Ezra, there is something you don't know. I haven't been trying to keep secrets from you. You know there's nobody I trust more than you. I just didn't know how to say this. Or when."

My mouth felt suddenly dry. "Nora, tell me."

She held my gaze and carefully pulled her mittens off, raising both palms for me to see. She turned her hands front to back . . . showing no scars on her perfectly formed fingers. "It wasn't me, Ezra."

I sighed.

"I don't know why the cops are at your grandparents' house. But I know what happened at the Schroeder fire now. You need to hear the whole story for it to make sense."

I pulled my gloves off and held both of her perfect hands in mine. "I need to know."

Our connection was abruptly severed by a sharp, ragged voice. A familiar one.

"I found you. I finally found you."

Nora and I both turned to the chilling sight of Matt Schroeder's pale blue eyes boring into us. His milk-white face looked pallid and haggard, except for the wide, bright pink scar on the left side of his face. He was wearing a greasy Carhartt jacket and his baseball hat. His thick, muscular hands gripped a large, red pipe wrench.

"Matt, don't do this. There's no need for anyone to get hurt," I said.

"Oh yes there is. Why do you think I didn't tell the cops who it was? I knew that if my dad was ever going to get justice, I'd have to do this myself."

"Nora, we need to get out of here *now*," I hissed.

Matt stepped into the access road, blocking our retreat back to the community center. The snow was too deep on the sides of the road to try to run anywhere else. Matt would have the pipe wrench on us before we got any distance away from him.

"Ezra, oh my God, what do we do?"

"Nora, we just have to get past him and run for help."

Just then I could see a familiar brown form rushing down the road toward us, behind Matt's back, his little claws tapping on the frozen road.

I yelled at the top of my voice, "Sic 'em, Buster!"

Buster yipped, and it was just enough to make Matt turn to see what was coming behind him. I lunged as hard and fast as I could at Matt, bowling him over from back to front, sprawling and sliding on the frozen road. Royce Gracie would have been proud.

"Run!"

Nora and I rushed past Matt, barreling down the road toward the community center.

"Buster, let's go!" The dog seemed willing to fight to the death with Matt Schroeder, but my voice pulled him out of the fight and brought him scurrying after us. Matt grabbed the pipe wrench and sprinted after us, enraged.

Our winter boots slowed us down even more than Matt's slippery tennis shoes slowed him, and he was closing behind us as we approached the sidewall of the community center. Buster started barking and I yelled at the top of my voice, "Dad!!"

We cornered the building at a full run. I could hear Matt huffing behind us and turned to see if he was close enough to strike. When I looked back in front of me, I saw a burst of brown movement and heard a loud baritone bellow.

My dad's enormous body barreled into Matt with such force that it made an audible crunch as they collided. The pipe wrench flew through the air and skidded into a snow bank. Matt Schroeder gave a loud grunt as the air was smacked out of his lungs. He spilled sideways and onto his back, blood jetting from his nose in rhythmic spurts. My dad's hand were clenched in fists as he towered over Matt's prostrate body. There was a flurry of motion after that as several men who had been sitting around Grandpa Liam's spirit fire jumped up and restrained both Matt and my father.

Someone ran down to my grandparents' house to get the RCMP. Within minutes, the RCMP and Detective Williams were on the scene. They arrested Matt and put him in the back of an RCMP squad car. Then they started taking statements from all the witnesses.

I really hoped my dad wouldn't be in trouble for knocking Matt Schroeder over. He was just protecting us.

When the squad car drove away with Matt, Detective Williams, a Corps Sergeant Major, and RCMP Superintendent pulled my dad into a conference. Nora and I stood behind him.

"Mr. Cloud," Detective Williams said. "Regarding this incident with Mr. Schroeder, we have determined that it is a clear case of self-defense. Schroeder had a weapon and was trying to hurt or kill your son and Nora George. You were protecting him. Our investigation won't be final until it's final, but for now, the RCMP won't be recommending any charges against you for striking him."

My dad nodded. A Native man hurting a white teenager didn't usually get that result, regardless of the circumstances. I felt relieved.

Williams continued, "And with regard to the Schroeder fire, we now have evidence that your father, Liam

Cloud, was likely responsible for starting the fire and holding the handle of the front door so the occupants could not escape."

My head was spinning. *That can't be right.*

"But that's impossible!" my dad interjected.

"You knew nothing about that?"

"I knew nothing. I don't even think it's true!" my dad said. He clenched his jaw, but he wrestled himself into composure, and didn't say anything more.

Mr. Williams continued, "I know this is hard to hear, Mr. Cloud. But we found receipts for cash purchases in his house that verify his travel to and presence in Minneapolis on the night of the fire. We also found a letter, in his own hand, confessing to both starting the fire and holding the door while the Schroeders perished inside. Apparently he was wearing heavy gloves, which explains why he didn't burn his hands. Your mother was at your house at the time, according to his letter. If that's the whole truth, he acted alone . . . no accomplices."

Grandpa Liam had directly told me that he didn't start the fire when we were back at the trapping cabin. I couldn't believe that was a lie. I could feel my blood pumping faster. "This can't be right," I murmured.

Detective Williams added, "I realize that it seems a little unlikely at first, but he was likely trying to protect your son, Ezra. The Schroeders obviously had some problems with him. Liam and Ezra were close. Please express our appreciation to Emma Cloud. When your mother reported this to us a couple days ago, all the pieces finally came together. We'll be issuing our final report soon and the case will be closed."

Detective Williams and the RCMP officers turned and left then. My dad looked at me in utter disbelief. I didn't know what to say either.

Nora and I followed my dad down the community center road to the main housing access road. None of us said a word. Nora was staring at her boots the whole time. My dad seemed to be staring off into space. I was trying to read their faces, but I felt as confused as ever. We stopped at Nora's to drop her off. My dad and I were planning to go home and ask Grandma Emma several pointed questions.

Before we could go, Nora took a deep breath and grabbed my hand. "Ezra, I think there's something else you need to see."

I had almost forgotten about our unfinished conversation after the commotion with Matt Schroeder and everything Detective Williams said.

"You too, Mr. Cloud."

My dad raised his eyebrows for a second, then we both followed Nora into her grandmother's house. We kicked off our boots and hung our coats by the door. Rita was in the kitchen already and motioned for everyone to sit at the table. She seemed to be expecting us.

Ruth came in a few moments later. Nora poured tea for everyone in awkward silence while her mom pulled a bannock pan out of the oven and placed it on the stove. Then Ruth sat at the table and pulled the oven mitts off her hands.

She turned them over to reveal the distinct discolored scars of a severe burn.

"No more secrets," she breathed. My dad and I looked at each other in shocked disbelief.

Nora spoke next, slow and deliberate. "On the night of the fire, I went for a walk. I was planning on coming to see if you were okay, Ezra, after what happened to your arm at school. I should have texted first, but I thought you might be sleeping. I didn't want to disturb you if you were resting and figured if you were, I could just go back. But I didn't even make it to your house. Matt Schroeder caught me on the sidewalk. I hadn't been thinking about him. He dragged me up the steps and into their house. I think they were going to hurt me . . . maybe even kill me. I was so scared. I screamed. I screamed while Matt pulled me in and I screamed inside. It's all I could do."

Ruth put her hand on Nora's arm and finished the story. "Nora is everything to me. I knew she was in trouble. The way Matt came after her at school was a big enough sign for me. But when she left our house without telling me what she was doing, I did what every mother eagle does when something's not right in the nest. I went after her. I heard her scream. I didn't even knock on the door. It wasn't locked, so I pushed it open and went after my girl."

Ruth took a long, slow inhale before she continued. "The fire wasn't arson. It was an accident. Matt was dragging Nora toward the basement stairs. I ran after them as fast as I could. Luke and Mark Schoeder were in the basement, but they heard Nora screaming and started up. The only reason we got out of there was because the stairs were just wide enough for Nora and I to fit side by side. We kicked and scratched and gouged and finally Matt let go. He tumbled down the stairs into Luke and Mark."

Ruth's voice quivered with emotion: "When they collided with each other, one of them must have knocked something over down there. There was a loud bang and a small explosion of some sort. Nora and I ran out the door right before the second explosion. A couple seconds slower, and we would have gone down in that house with the Schroeders."

I glanced at Nora. The memory of that night alone still put a look of fear on her face.

Ruth finished: "I told Nora to run home as fast as she could. Then . . . I went back. I was scared of the Schroeders, but I didn't want anyone to get hurt. I thought I should help them get out. I tried to open the front door, but the handle was so hot that it burned through my skin before I could even turn it. I never saw any of the Schroeders. I didn't even know Matt survived until later. He must have crawled out of a basement window before the whole house came down. He obviously saw me. In the dark and from the back, I look a lot like Nora. When he accosted you the next day, I think he thought Nora held the door shut on purpose. But it was actually me trying to help them get out."

"How did you avoid the cops finding out you burned your hands?" I blurted out.

"They interviewed the kids from the school who knew Matt, but they didn't interview all their parents."

Rita spoke up then: "When your Grandpa Liam was in the hospital and knew that he wasn't going to make it, he decided that if any of the Clouds or Georges had anything to do with the fire, he would take responsibility. I told everything I knew to Emma during one of my visits to the hospital. She did what Liam asked. Emma called the authorities to report him. He wrote a letter confessing to the crime. He had someone put the receipts in their house that would back everything up. I think he wanted to spare us all losing a family member to the system."

Nora's voice had a slight tremble of emotion. "He saved my mom."

My gaze shifted around the table to my dad, Rita, Ruth, and finally Nora. I looked at her beautiful eyes, glowing in the filtered winter light streaming into the kitchen, before I added, "He saved us all."

Chapter 30

THE GRAVESITE was located at the mouth of the Otter-tail River on the shore of Rainy Lake. It had an auspicious view of the lake, all the way up toward Porter's Inlet and the bays we traveled to get to Chief's Ridge. The picturesque rock escarpments and crags were lined with balsam, black spruce, and red, white, and jack pine, with pristine waterways extending forth in all directions. In the summer months, this was where we came to fish, and the entire waterway from Ottertail Lake to the bays of Rainy abounded in in walleye pike, muskellunge, crappie, and smallmouth bass.

The area was showing the first signs of the spring breakup and ice melt. Winter's hand would soon release its grip and give way to the verdant growth and prosperity of spring. My dad and I came before first light on the morning of Grandpa Liam's funeral to dig the grave.

It was our custom to dig the grave on the day of the funeral so the hole was only open long enough to claim one body. It could invite bad luck to dig the day before. Digging at the mouth of the Ottertail River was a hard job under any circumstances. The river was deeper here long ago, and the gravesite was part of the original riverbed, full of rocks, gravel, and roots, all packed with clay. We had one long shovel, one short shovel, and a pick ax. The ax did most of the work. We built a fire in the predawn dark and let it burn down to coals first so it would melt the snow and frost. Then we started to dig.

The work was slow, but we took turns with the ax and excavated with steady determination. I tried not to think about my mom's gravesite just a few yards away, or lowering Grandpa Liam's body into this hole when we were done. The work kept me from shivering, but my feet and hands were numb with cold. The wet clay and melted snow penetrated my pants, socks, and boots.

Finally, we finished digging, lowered in the rough box that would receive Grandpa's casket after the funeral, and stood at the base of the grave, aching with cold and bottled emotion. I thought about the story Grandpa Liam shared with me on the banks of Manidookaan and turned to my dad.

"Grandpa Liam told me about Ethan and Olivia."

My dad lifted his head and our eyes locked. He waited a moment, then said, "I'm so glad he shared that story with you."

"Yeah." There were more words in my heart, but I couldn't find them.

My dad leaned on the long shovel and kept looking at me. "I think he waited his whole adult life to discharge that pain. It makes it easier to deal with my own. I was so young when they were taken that I barely remember them, and my memories are like pictures, rather than the full tapestry of life we should have shared."

He brought his sleeve to his face and wiped the water from his nose. "I never set foot inside Carlisle Indian Industrial School, Haskell, Tomah, Kamloops, or Brandon—not as a student, and not even as a visitor. But I've been fighting the demons they unleashed my whole life. We all have."

I felt a low, aching feeling in my heart thinking about the sacrifices made and injustices endured by Ethan, Olivia, Grandpa Liam, Grandma Emma, and my dad. I looked at him standing there in the graveyard, soaked to the bone, smeared with muddy clay and melting snow. Whether it was the ordeals we had been through with

my mom, the fire, the bear, or Grandpa Liam's passing—
or Grandpa's words echoing in my ear—I let my eyes see
him in new light, traveling from his taciturn face to his
muscular shoulders to his large, long, clumsy fingers.
There was blood trickling from a fresh gash on his right
hand, likely caused by one of the roots we'd had to chop
through digging the grave.

I fell to my knees. I had hardly spoken to my dad for
the better part of a year, except to express my anger and
disapproval. The lumber mill took his wife, and now the
wilderness took his dad. He had been so worried about
losing me through it all. I had been so blind and so
ungrateful. For some people, fear and loss close their
hearts, leaving them guarded and lonely and discon-
nected. But somehow, they opened me.

Kneeling in the snow and frozen mud near my
grandfather's grave, I found my voice. I was ready to tell
him everything—that I would never hurt myself or anyone else; that I was done being a sulky, angry omega
and I was ready to join the pack; that I would lead it
someday, and he would have many grandchildren; that
I was so sorry for my behavior, for Grandpa Liam, for
everything; that I loved him with my whole heart.

I rose to my feet and looked him in the eyes and
my voice started to rumble, deep in my chest, growing
and strengthening, then gushing forth. But instead of a

well-worded soliloquy, my voice caught in my throat and lofted in the winter sky as a high-pitched howl and a torrent of tears. My chest heaved uncontrollably as I cried and cried. He folded me into a tight embrace.

"There has never been a father who loved his son as much as I love you, Ezra."

And I believed him.

My voice must have carried on the winter wind. Off in the distance, a wolf howled. And another. And then a chorus filled the sky. For the first time in my life, I really felt at home. Home, with the winter wind whistling through the pines, driving the tears from my face, and whipping at my hair. Home, in the faith that the earth would claim my grandpa's body, but his spirit would live eternal. Home, in the hope of Nora's love. Home, in my father's big, brown, beautiful hands. Home, right here, where wolves don't die.

Ojibwe Translations

Aandego-giizis — Crow Moon

Abin omaa, gwis. — Sit here, son.

Adikokan — Caribou Bone

Anangoowinini — Star Man

Awesiinyensag — Little Animals

Bebookwaagime-giizis — Broken Snowshoe Moon

Chi-awesiinh — Big animal

Gaawiin. Indinenimaag abinoojiinyag ayaanzigwaa gegoo ji-miijiwaad. — No. I am thinking of children with nothing to eat.

Gaawiin. Indinenimaag gichi-aya'aag gashkitoosigwaa ji-bami'idizowaad. — No. I am thinking of the elders who aren't able to provide for themselves.

Gaawiin. Indinenimaag indinaawemaaganag, niijanishinaabeg, miinawaa gaa-pi-izhaajig ji-wiidookawiwaad. — No. I am thinking of my family members, my community members, and those who came here today to support me.

Gego agonwetawaaken! Gidaa-debweyenimaa. — Don't doubt him! You should believe in him.

Gidishpenimin, we'! — I am proud of you, namesake!

Gimikwenimaanaanig gidinawemaaganinaanig gaa-aandakiijig. — We remember our relatives who have changed worlds.

Gwis — Son

Indinawemaaganidog, odaapinaadaa wa'aw asemaa! Oshkinitaage Anangoowinini. — My relatives, accept this tobacco. Star Man has made his first kill.

Indinawemaaganidog, onjida gigiiwitaabimin. Ani-ininiiwi noozhishenh. — My relatives, we sit here with a purpose. My grandson is becoming a man.

Manidoog — The spirits

Manidookaan — The Place of Spirits

Miigwech — Thank you

Miigwech aapiji zhawenimiyan. Onjida inga-aabajitoon giwiiyaas ji-bami'agwaa niijanishinaabeg. Gaawiin inga-nishwanaajitoosiin giiyaw. — Thank you so much for pitying me. I will use your meat for the purpose of providing for my fellow Natives.

Miigwech zhawenimiyan. Gibiindaakoonin weweni. — Thank you for pitying me. I offer you tobacco in a good way.

Mino-bawaajigen! — Dream well!

Nigigoonsiminikaaning — The Place Where There Are a
  Lot of Little Otter Berries

Noozhishenh — My grandchild

Ogimaa — Chief

Onaabani-giizis — Crusted Snow Moon

Author's Note

WHERE WOLVES DON'T DIE is a work of fiction. The places are real, including Northeast Minneapolis, International Falls, Fort Frances, Nigigoonsiminikaaning First Nation, Ottertail River, Red Gut Bay, Atikokan, and the trapping area. The details of houses and cabins and some of the geographical details on the trapline, including the name Chief's Ridge, are my creation and not intended to represent anyone's actual home or private property. The story of Adikokan is largely true, including it being a caribou graveyard, but details of the anthropology and archaeology there are altered for storytelling effect.

My son Evan is an enrolled member of the Nigigoonsiminikaaning First Nation. We live at Leech Lake and our family has lived and been buried there since long before America became a country. I am a descendant of Leech Lake, White Earth, Mille Lacs, and Red Lake Ojibwe families. My mother and grandmother were enrolled at White Earth. My grandfather was enrolled at Leech Lake. Because of our bloodlines and family connections to these and other places in this book, and my work officiating ceremonies throughout Ojibwe country, it is also important to share that all the characters in this book are fiction and not based on or reflective of any actual living human being.

At Red Gut, the immediate family typically does not dig the grave. Other families and friends dig the grave by hand for the bereaved there. The scene in the final chapter was described that way for narrative impact rather than as a cultural explanation.

I too come from a large family of Native hunters, trappers, and harvesters whose woodsy knowledge shaped me in many ways. This book is fiction, but it is not simply an imagining of, but a window into Native harvesting, ceremony, and coming of age as I have been taught by many people, including my mother, Margaret Treuer; cousins Mike and Bobby Matthews; uncles David, Sonny, and Lanny Seelye; stepfather, Ron LaFriniere; my namesake, Mary Roberts; and my chiefs and spiritual leaders Archie Mosay, Tom Stillday, Anna Gibbs, Melvin Eagle, Dora Ammann, and Jim Clark. I'd also like to thank the Allen and Jones families at Red Gut, especially Dan and Dennis Jones who have taken me hunting and fishing there since the early 1990s, and all of their families, including but not limited to Josephine, Marie, Nancy, Gail, Jason, Travis, Carmen, Shawna, and Don.

I am deeply indebted to many people for their help, advice, and support in the creation of this book. Thank you to my children Elias, Evan, Mia, and Luella who listened to me read it out loud in drafts for their advice and comment, and my other children Madeline, Robert, Caleb, Isaac, and Jordan who supported all my time and effort devoted to writing this. And special thanks to my wife, Blair, who has had to share me with our people and my career and creative ambition with such patience, love, and grace.

About the Author

Greene Photography

DR. ANTON TREUER (pronounced troy-er) is Professor of Ojibwe at Bemidji State University and author of many books. His professional work in education, history, and Indigenous studies and long service as an officiant at Ojibwe tribal ceremonies have made him a consummate storyteller in the Ojibwe cultural tradition and a well-known public speaker. In 2018, he was named Guardian of Culture and Lifeways and recipient of the Pathfinder Award by the Association of Tribal Archives, Libraries, and Museums. Anton's first book for young adults, *Everything You Wanted to Know About Indians But Were Afraid to Ask (Young Readers Edition),* won the SCBWI Golden Kite. This is his first novel.

Some Notes on This Book's Production

The art for the jacket, case, and interiors was drawn digitally
by Mangeshig Pawis-Steckley (Anishinaabe/Ojibwe, Wasauksing
First Nation) using Procreate, stylized in an Anishinaabe woodland
art style. The text was set by Westchester Publishing Services,
in Danbury, CT, in Meridien, a typeface designed in 1957
by Swiss designer Adrien Frutiger for Deberny & Peignot.
Frutiger based it off of Nicolas Jenson's 16th-century characters
and sought to create something extremely legible and aesthetically
pleasing. The book was printed on FSCTM-certified 78gsm
Yunshidai Ivory paper and bound in China.

Production supervised by Freesia Blizard
Book designed by Patrick Collins
Assistant Managing Editor: Danielle Maldonado
Editor: Nick Thomas

LEVINE QUERIDO